Sophia James lives in Chelsea Bay, on Auckland, New Zealand's North Shore, with her husband, who is an artist. She has a degree in English and History from Auckland University and believes her love of writing was formed by reading Georgette Heyer in the holidays at her grandmother's house. Sophia enjoys getting feedback at Facebook.com/sophiajamesauthor.

Also by Sophia James

A Secret Consequence for the Viscount
Their Marriage of Inconvenience
'Christmas with the Earl'
in *Christmas Cinderellas*
The Spinster's Scandalous Affair
The Debutante's Secret

Gentlemen of Honour miniseries

A Night of Secret Surrender
A Proposition for the Comte
The Cinderella Countess

Secrets of a Victorian Household collection

Miss Lottie's Christmas Protector

Discover more at millsandboon.co.uk.

SCANDALOUS NIGHTS WITH THE EARL

Sophia James

MILLS & BOON

First published in Great Britain 2025
by Mills & Boon, an imprint of HarperCollins*Publishers* Ltd,
1 London Bridge Street, London, SE1 9GF

www.harpercollins.co.uk

HarperCollins*Publishers*, Macken House, 39/40 Mayor Street Upper,
Dublin 1, D01 C9W8, Ireland

ISBN: 978-0-263-34537-7

10/25

FSC
www.fsc.org
MIX
Paper | Supporting responsible forestry
FSC™ C007454

This book contains FSC™ certified paper
and other controlled sources to ensure responsible forest management.

For more information visit www.harpercollins.co.uk/green.

Printed and Bound in the UK using 100% Renewable Electricity
at CPI Group (UK) Ltd, Croydon, CR0 4YY

This story is for Rafael, Rome, Beau and Ashton,
my honourable, brave and kind young heroes.

Chapter One

Hampshire, England. 1820

Phillip James Kellan Moreland, the eighth Earl of Elmsworth, arrived at his estate in Hampshire just after midday on a cold May afternoon, the wind up and heavy rain pooling on the ground. He could barely look at the place, dark against a leaden sky, the crenulated palisades of stone even more unwelcoming than they had been when he'd left, four years prior.

Home.

The very word made him frown.

His younger brother was no longer in residence. He'd had a letter from Oliver a few years earlier explaining that his personal circumstances had changed substantially and because of it he had installed a farm manager at Elmsworth in his stead. The accounts Phillip had looked over briefly in London before returning to Hampshire had shown that the manager was doing a fine job, and he was thankful for such an easy turn of fortune. Still, he had little heart to be here again.

Gretel, his wife, was dead. Lying under a gravestone four thousand miles away, the earth of another land all around her.

Fisting his fingers, he breathed in hard, glad at least for the solitude and seclusion Elmsworth would bring. He did not wish for conversation, laughter or questions. He did not want to hear once again from some well-meaning soul about how time healed loss and made living easier.

'Everyone can master a grief but he that has it.'

He remembered these words from his schooling years at Eton. For a while, they had been etched into the wood of a drawer base by the side of his bed. He had put them there himself with the sharp point of his knife, Miranda Moreland's last letter resting on top.

Mama's instability had baffled him until finally he'd had enough, and he'd made a paper plane of her last tangled missive on returning home one summer and sent the nonsense into the pond she had drowned in. Oliver had been more sensible, Phillip thought then, for his brother had read his letter once and then burnt it. He had no idea as to what had happened to his father's.

All he did know was that his mother's sickness had reached out to hurt each of them years after her death and turned them all into people they had not wanted to be.

'Thun-der-ation.' He said the word slowly, breaking it into the same drawn-out syllables they seemed to favour in the American south. But there was no sense in wallowing in all that he had hated here, and at the age of almost thirty-three it was far past time to move on. The sombre sameness of the place brought everything back, that was the trouble, the inescapable sense of doom making him uneasy. He knew he had been called the Arrogant Earl in Society because of his distaste for the constant expectations. But tradition was a hard taskmaster and with the Moreland blood flowing in his veins he had no other pathway available to him but to return to England and make the best of it.

His attention was caught by a carriage that stood on the circular driveway before the manor, looking to all intents and purposes as if it had just arrived. There were two footmen hovering around the back of the conveyance and a driver was at the front checking on the team of horses whose breath was steaming in the cold.

Visitors. Now? He swore as he stepped down from his own carriage and walked into the house to be met by a group of elderly females all fanned around a younger one lying prostrate on the long sofa in the green salon just off the entrance hall. He could not see her face but the expressions on those beside her told him there had been some sort of major mishap.

Mrs King, his housekeeper, turned and saw him first, a comical expression of shock widening her eyes and her mouth falling open.

'My Lord Elmsworth? You are returned home at last?' Disbelief lay in every word.

The other elderly ladies instantly looked across as well, three sets of identical watery blue eyes fixed upon him.

'Indeed I have. Is there a problem here, Mrs King?'

The young woman lying down was now visible. Her cheeks were pale and her eyes reddened. As she recognised his presence, consternation appeared on her face. She tried to sit up, swivelling her feet to the floor, and her complexion became paler still.

'I would lie down again if I were you, Miss…?'

He waited as one of the older women furnished her name.

'Mrs St Claire, Lord Elmsworth.'

'And… I am…never…sick.'

This quiet rejoinder from the patient had him observing her more closely. It was true. She did not give the appearance of one of the thin, pale and fragile butterflies Society lauded. She was curvaceous, the line of her bodice showing off a generous bosom. He felt a hot and unfamiliar flicker of interest inside and it shocked him.

'Well, you are indeed most ill now, my dear.' The ancient woman nearest to her said this.

'Because the meal last night…was tainted.' The patient's glance met his own, direct and honest and with a good sprinkling of horror within it.

'She has been sick all night, my lord, and then three times again this morning. She is so sick she cannot keep anything down at all, which is why we called in to your estate for help.'

'But… I…am…feeling better…'

Phillip saw her chin tremble even as she said it and tried to school the scowl he knew to be on his own face.

'You should rest for a while.'

The words sounded sharp and short but even as he uttered them her breathing changed, the old woman standing closest grabbing at the bowl on the table and the visitor's head disappearing as she heaved violently into it.

'Mrs King, could I have a private word with you?'

'Of course, sir.'

After making sure they could not be overheard from this far down the passage Phillip spoke softly. 'If the St Claire party needs to stay tonight, offer them a place to lay down their heads. I will leave it to you to see that they are gone in the morning.'

'Yes, sir.'

He left then, striding through to his library with intent. God, he did not need another sick woman around him. Gretel's malady had lingered on and on, until even she was tired of her inability to find peace at the end of it.

There was brandy in the cabinet. His brother had always been an expert on good liquor and Phillip was pleased for the four bottles of vintage cognac lined up on the shelf.

Finding a glass and opening a bottle, he poured himself a liberal amount. It was good, he thought next, the smooth taste improving his mood. He'd stay in here till the unwanted group were either departed or settled upstairs and that surely could not be too far away. With resolve he lifted one of the many heavy farm ledgers down from the shelf behind him and began to read.

The man who had just left was the most beautiful male Wilhelmina Evelyn St Claire had ever seen in her entire life. Oh, she knew beauty to be a fleeting and shallow thing, and such physical blessings should hardly make a difference to one's worth, and yet for some reason this man's looks had her normally far more sensible heart beating at a pace that was worrying. The fact that such an unexpected Adonis had seen her at her very worst, head in the ceramic basin bringing up that dreadful chicken pie purchased last night from the inn on the road towards London, was something she could hardly change. So she simply lay back and admitted defeat.

She knew who he was, of course she did. Mr Phillip Moreland, the eighth Earl of Elmsworth may have been unpopular in Society because of his arrogance but nobody had ever disputed his beauty. She just had not expected his eyes, that was all, filled with a sadness and a sense of guilt that had made the scowl on his face less alarming somehow. He had his demons, for sure, but he also had that particular and familiar grief that loss left marked upon his body with a howling truth.

He had loved his wife. She had heard that said many times, the beautiful, ethereal, slight and pale Miss Gretel Carmichael, a debutante who had conquered her season like no other woman had before or since. A love match. Rare. Exceptional. Extraordinary.

Her own marriage had been nothing like that.

She could hear the McAllistair sisters talking with the housekeeper. The woman was offering their party rooms for the night, and the chance to recover in comfort until they resumed their journey across to London on the morrow. She stated firmly that it would be of no inconvenience whatsoever.

Did the Earl of Elmsworth know such arrangements were being suggested? Willa doubted he would, which in itself was intriguing. Given that the servant did not fear reprisals for such a proposal, she could only assume that Lord Elmsworth was not a master who ruled his roost with an exacting and formidable iron fist. If she had felt even a smidgeon better she would have refused the offer and got back in the carriage, but the waves of nausea were not leaving her and she felt too wrung out for an argument. The long journey to London was too much to consider and sitting upright and constrained in a moving vehicle would be the very definition of impossible. She wanted darkness and silence. She wanted to be in a prone position with a soft pillow beneath her aching head and the chance of complete and utter stillness.

She also wanted desperately to be away from the unending and shrill chatter of the three elderly McAllistair sisters.

Swallowing back the tears she could feel welling behind her eyes, she took in a deep breath. She hardly ever cried and almost never felt overwhelmed by circumstance, for eleven years with a difficult husband had cured her forever of passionate feeling. When Lionel had slipped off the balcony and died she had simply tidied him up and called the undertaker before making arrangements for his burial. Then she had left Belton Park and never returned until this journey, taken to dispose of unwanted possessions before the sale of the property. After Lionel's passing she had made a troth to live every subsequent day in her life as if it was her last and she had made a fine job of such a promise thus far.

Well, not today, obviously. Her stomach growled and the ceramic bowl wiped with strong alcohol and mint made her heave.

She felt like death. She wished she were home in her rented town house in London. She wished her companions were all returned to their shared abode and that she could be completely by herself with no one at all to see her or hear her.

Then she might be able to cry properly, she mused, that observation so ridiculous that she smiled for the first time in hours. One day this might all seem like an amusing story, the gloriously handsome Earl of Elmsworth, her plight, the basin, the competent servant and the three fussing old sisters. But right at this moment, it was not even remotely humorous.

She wondered where Phillip Moreland had disappeared to and hoped that she would not see him again before she left Elmsworth, which would be as early as feasible on the morrow.

It was late. The clock had just chimed out the hour of two and Phillip knew he should be making an effort for bed and sleep, but he felt out of kilter and restless.

The cognac had knocked the edge off his tiredness and this house, for all its faults, was a solid enough place when set against the rising north-west wind. He had returned home without servants and so he had no one to answer to, which was a relief, though the housekeeper had been here a few hours ago informing him of the presence overnight of the unexpected guests and asking if he would like a manservant sent up to see him to bed.

He'd refused and instructed her not to have a servant remain to attend to him. He had been largely alone during his last two years' travelling around America and had grown to appreciate the lack of being beholden to anyone for anything.

But he was hungry after partaking in his study of

an early dinner and Mrs King had informed him that there was bread and cheese left out on the bench if he did find himself with an appetite in the middle of the night.

The kitchen was fairly dim when he walked in but a movement to his left had him turning, and there, standing very still, was the young woman who had been the patient this afternoon. She looked completely different. A little pale still perhaps but greatly recovered, a dressing gown pulled tightly in and her hair down.

It was the colour of autumn, browns and reds and blackness curling thickly to her waist. For a second he wondered what it would feel like to run his fingers through such abundance and was disorientated by the thought. Gretel's hair had been pale and thin, and, threaded as it was in gold and white, she had never been able to grow it past her shoulders as much as she had tried.

The surprise of seeing him here was in her eyes, darkened by the lack of light.

'I am sorry, Lord Elmsworth. I was hungry and so I came down. I will leave.'

'No.' The word stopped her and he wondered why he had said it with such force. 'I need to eat, too, and there is cheese and bread here. Would you like some?'

Her smile was immediate.

'I would, indeed.'

The lack of hesitation heartened him, for he'd never had time for the wiles of women. His wife had been direct as well.

He watched the stranger pull her night attire closer as she sat, a careful movement with slight embarrassment evident and a large dollop of wariness. She obviously knew of his reputation but it felt good to have someone to talk with on the first night of his long-overdue return to Elmsworth Manor. A scent of gardenias wafted around her.

'You look much healthier than you did this morning, at least.'

She blushed at that and he wondered if such words were a misstep.

'I could not look worse even if I'd tried, my lord.'

'Phillip,' he gave back. His time in the Americas had allowed him to understand that the fussy insistence on titles and manners was rather outdated.

'Phillip,' she returned. 'And I am Wilhelmina. My companions and I stopped at a tavern on the road, The King's Way, I think it was called, and they served chicken pie for supper. No one else got ill save for me, which in its own way is a blessing, given the age and frailty of my three travelling companions.'

'Where were you coming from?'

'My husband's estate outside of Winchester. He died just over two years ago.'

'I am very sorry.'

She looked at him then and frowned. 'Thank you, but I suppose I should also say that ours was not a love match. By the end of our union Lionel, that was his name, liked me as little as I liked him.'

'Lionel?'

'Mr Lionel St Claire from Belton Park. He was a friend of my parents' and he was lonely.'

'And in the end you were, too?'

She laughed so unexpectedly it made him smile. 'The lesson I learned was that one should not marry to make others happy.'

'I hope you have better luck next time, then.'

'Oh, there will not be a next time, I can assure you of that. One thing my husband did possess was wealth and he has left me an independent widow of some means, which is an enormous relief after the constrictions of those lost eleven years.'

'A fair amount of time?' He liked her returned humour.

'Too much entirely but there was no one else to blame, for it was my own mistake. Had I been like other young girls with dreams of more I might have waited and made a better match.'

'But you did not?'

'Mama and Papa were scientists. Their world was of insects and habitats, all practical and rational things. So in effect mine was, too.'

'And Lionel?'

'Loved astronomy. He was well regarded in his field but the smallness of the earth in the universe depressed him and he could never be happy. In the end I think he was largely irritated because I could be. It pays not to think too much of the inequalities in this world, you see, my lord, for in reality all the worry in the heavens will not change anything save to leave one with a spiralling anxiety and an ever-present dread.'

She nibbled at the bread and cheese as she said this. Phillip noticed her fingers were long, her nails short and neat.

'I decided a long time ago to simply be content with my own company, you see, and so far such a resolution has worked out well. If it were not for the infamous chicken pie, I should now be in London in my town house, scouring the shelves of my library for the next wonderful story to read.'

'You enjoy books, then?'

'Immensely. I love the places one can escape to

within them. When I was married escape was… more difficult. Lionel thought a woman's work in her house should never be done and even a speck of dust annoyed him. It was a very large house and so there was bound to be some encroaching detritus that blew in no matter how hard one endeavoured to banish it, but he was not a husband who enjoyed paying servants for doing the jobs he thought a wife should manage.'

Phillip could not remember a time when he had spoken to a female of such candour. Mrs St Claire was a woman who did not embroider things and one who owned up to the mistakes she had made with a quiet truth. In this she was like no other woman he had met. But she wasn't yet finished.

'I always think it rather an odd thing that one must be forever on one's best behaviour in a relationship. A quiet, restful acceptance of each other would have been far more to my liking but Lionel had other, more brittle wants, and his constant needs were of no help to me at all. I think had he been born a monk he might have been more at peace with himself. A different life so to speak and one where he needed to make no human contact.'

'The mantra of solitude?'

'You know of these teachings, then?'

'Once I did.'

He had not meant to give such raw truths but her honesty had made him less wary than he usually was. Biting down on other words, he tried to find a balance.

Lord Elmsworth watched her with uncertainty. She had probably been far more honest than she ought but all those silent years with Lionel had taught her the value of words. Besides, she would never see the earl again after this, for was it not said that the Moreland men always were seen with the most beautiful women in the Ton on their arms?

She was reasonably plain, a little overweight and far too old to be thought desirable, so this midnight supper in an ancient family pile with the most handsome man in all the world was a moment out of time and one which would never be repeated.

There was an ease in such knowledge. Changing the subject, she sought for a lighter topic.

'Your house is a very interesting place and, even given my poor health on arrival, I saw some of the views as we swept down the drive, and they were vistas, by the way, that were in every direction spectacular. Have you always lived here?'

'Up until the last few years I have.'

'Your housekeeper said that you have recently been in America and I certainly hope it is not the biggest of inconveniences to have us here. We will be gone by mid-morning at the latest, I promise. It would be sooner if our departure time was left solely to me but I doubt the McAllistair sisters are early risers and so…'

'Are they relatives of yours?'

'No, but they are old friends who were very kind to me when I first arrived in London. Their father was Lord McAllistair but he died at least ten years ago, and though the townhouse that they reside in is tithed to a male cousin the man has not yet come forward with his hope to claim it.'

She stopped as she saw him smile.

'I am talking too much? I try not to but when I am nervous I do so without even realising.'

'Are you nervous?'

'I am, for I know that we are a dull and drab group and one you could hardly be thrilled to have ensconced so unexpectedly in your splendid residence overnight.'

'You seem to have heard a lot about me.'

'Most of it is hearsay, I do assure you, though once, years and years ago, I did walk close to you at the Merryweather ball in Mayfair.'

He'd been dressed almost entirely in black and as she had passed him in the smaller salon off the main one he had caught her eye. At the time she had felt as if she had been seared in hot water, her skin reddening and her heart pounding, for it was not often anyone truly noticed her, and especially not someone like the beautiful Phillip Moreland. She remembered scrambling back to her husband and taking his arm, an intimacy she very rarely displayed but Moreland had unsettled her with his smile and made her realise all the things she might have missed out on if she had only waited for a husband with more to offer her than Lionel had.

Tonight she knew her place though, her advancing age and simple looks holding an anchor to a reality that was so much easier.

'I seldom liked Society events,' he said. 'In fact I came down to London in the last years only occasionally before I left England for America.' He looked at her and carried on. 'My wife was sick.'

'I had heard that and I am sorry for it.'

'She died two and a half years ago in Richmond, Virginia, cradled in the arms of her mother.'

'That sounds peaceful.'

'It wasn't.'

The clock in the corner marked the seconds of silence. Further away outside Willa could hear a barn owl screeching. For prey. A field mouse perhaps or a vole. Inside the voluminous kitchen of Elmsworth the fire in the stove crackled, flames throwing shadows against the wall. The Earl looked as if he regretted all the truths he had given her and so she tried to find a new angle to their conversation.

'Are you of the persuasion, my lord, that people who are dead can look down upon us from the afterlife and see what we are up to?'

'I most certainly am not.'

She liked his reply because it was real and faintly shocked. When he did not speak again, she did.

'You were lucky to find a wife who suited you so entirely and I am sure she must have felt that way, too. If my late husband were to observe me from his place in the afterworld he would no doubt be most displeased.'

'And why would that be, Mrs St Claire?'

'Because rules and manners and absurdly strict social mores are things I no longer care to adhere to.'

'You are a rebel?'

'No, I think that word holds too much anger. I would describe myself as wishing to simply be happy, which in itself is a much gentler life choice.'

'And are you? Simply happy?'

She looked at him closely, seeing the chips of blue in his eyes smudged by silver. 'Yes, I think I am.'

A bolt of heat raced through Phillip, a feeling so unfamiliar he momentarily felt dizzy.

Her eyes were not just gold. There was copper there, too, and traces of hazel, and under the boldness sat a question. The question of possibility? Phillip could not believe she might mean it as such as he sought to diffuse his shock.

'Happiness is a much undervalued commodity, I think.' And he meant what he said, though the words in this context seemed at best trite.

'You say that as if perhaps you have known too much sorrow.'

'There are varying degrees of sadness, Mrs St Claire. A husband who was so unsuitable must have left you with at least some sense of melancholy.'

She nodded, the thickness of her dark hair coming forward. 'It did, indeed, but it was an experience that made me decide after Lionel was gone not to waste the chances presented to me for the rest of my years.'

'Chances?' The blood pounded in his head.

'I take delight in life where I find it and without apology.' Her glance was direct and candid.

'You are most brave, Mrs St Claire, and I admire you for it. Do you take these chances often?'

She smiled then but did not answer. The folds of fabric in her gown seemed loosened, whether by accident or design he could not tell, but the pale glow of the skin at her neck was beguiling.

He moved his left hand to his thigh and felt the

grip of it. There was a dimple in the middle of her chin and her lips were full and shapely. Once, years ago, when first they had married, Gretel had made an effort to look interested in the act of sexual attraction, but after a little while…

Comparisons were unhelpful and unfair. He didn't quite know what to say in return but couldn't leave it, either.

'Do you think that such risk is always a wise thing?'

She laughed. 'One never knows until one tries it, I suppose.'

He heard the siren's voice in her answer even as desire ran through him but he was not a man who could let sense go so entirely.

'Just before my wife died she asked me to be faithful to her memory.'

'Forever?'

'Yes. I think that was the gist of it.'

'What a horrible request.'

He began to laugh and thought as he did so that the sound felt rusty. 'You are not a believer, then, in the concept of eternal love, Mrs St Claire?'

She shook her head. 'Oh, on the contrary, my lord, should there be in this world a man who would suit me eternally I would relish it. But I think it highly unlikely.'

'How so?'

'Because I am not looking for such permanency. My friends would tell you I shy away from any commitment whatsoever and it is a truth, but after living with a man who was unsuitable in every way possible one becomes careful.'

'Careful to never choose again?'

'Careful to make sure that the choices are my own.' She frowned. 'I am amazed I am speaking of this, given that you might be a man who likes to gossip.'

'How little you know of me,' he returned and looked her in the eye. 'The Elmsworth name has always been on the sharp edge of scandal and it makes one cautious in any conversation. For years I never went near the city because of rumours that were loudly stated.'

'The stories about your family?'

'It seems you have heard them.'

'I should imagine if I'd listened to the gossip about my marriage it would have been equally damning.'

'But you didn't listen?'

'I didn't.'

Phillip was thrown off centre, spiralling to a place he hadn't found himself in before. He had been so long out of Society he felt…discomforted.

When he failed to speak her left hand moved to

cup her chin as she leaned forward. There was no ring on her fourth finger, which was both telling and appropriate. He almost wished he might strip his own off just for now, but such an action seemed disloyal.

Gretel. Her face was faded and blurred in the heat of a different need. He felt like another man, a freer one, a man who might step outside duty and memory for one moment and live.

'What do your friends call you, Mrs St Claire?'

'Willa.'

Her hand bumped across his on the table as she resettled herself at the kitchen bench, though she was careful to move it away. Touch was a beguiling thing, he thought next. It had been two and a half years since he had felt another's skin against his own and Wilhelmina St Claire was warm. Gretel's fingers had always been cold, some affliction of circulation she had had since childhood. His own shook slightly and he swore under his breath as he tried to still them.

'Which hand do you write with, my lord?'

Another unexpected question? He could barely keep up.

'My right.'

'Then I shall read your left one. Cup it slightly

like this near the candle. Good.' He felt her glance upon him.

'This is your head line and it tells me that you mull over things for a long time.' Her finger hovered above his palm. 'Your heart line has a cross on it.' She stopped.

'Which means?'

'You have experienced a deep and personal betrayal…'

He jerked back abruptly before she could say more but she only smiled, holding out her own left hand.

'Mine is the same but with even more crosses. Lionel is one of those, to be sure, and my parents are probably another, but these ones… I don't know about their meaning and perhaps I never will. The truth is these things are only a pathway to what we don't want to be.'

The light of the candle on her face made her skin glow.

'You are saying, then, that the lines of the body have their own stories?' Even as he phrased this question he wondered where it had come from. He had always been so rational and practical but he felt as if he had been transported inside the Garden of Eden and to the beginning of the world.

She did not do what he expected. She did not adhere to rules. She was nothing like Gretel. Worry thundered in his head and he swallowed.

'It has been a long time since…' He could not finish, could not put into words exactly what he was thinking as he touched the gold ring encircling his fourth finger.

Such actions left him vulnerable, for Willa St Claire would be able to see the effect she had on him and it was right that she should. He had never strayed, not once in all the years of his marriage, not even after Gretel was gone. He had never had a mistress or used the services of a courtesan while he had been married to her either here in England or in the Americas, and so it had been a long time since such physical closeness had been his.

'I have never been disloyal even to the memory of my wife.'

His words were honest, for this rush of lust was an unquiet thing.

'She was lucky, then.'

The length of her hair fell forward like a rope as she said these words, like a mythical goddess fashioned in flesh.

'Hell.' The curse escaped because for this moment on this night under a passing storm he felt lighter. He wanted to kiss Wilhelmina St Claire but he understood that of course he could not and should not.

So instead he took her hand, warm and fragile in his own, and simply held it, liking the way her fingers curled up to reach for him.

His blue eyes were rimmed in silver and if she saw questions there he did not voice them.

He held her as if she were made of glass, a brittle and fragile thing, easily broken. Outside the wind was loud but in here the crackle of the kitchen hearth fire was gentler.

A house that had withstood sorrows and change. Willa had heard so much said of the Elmsworth lords in Society that it was hard to believe even half of it.

And yet the truth of Phillip Moreland's hurt was here, in his silence and stillness. So much so that she sought to help him.

'When you allow the past the power to mould you it is difficult to find a future.' Her words were softly said as he pulled his hand away.

'There were times when I barely wanted one…' He stopped at that, his body rigid as he stood. 'I should not be here speaking to you of these things and alone at night…'

'Because it is easier to live with grief than to imagine something different?'

'Easier and safer, Mrs St Claire.'

At that she stood too, seared in the shock of what

was erupting inside of her. She had never felt like this before, never felt the aching thrust of pure want rush across sense, and it scared her.

'You are so very beautiful.' The words came from her unbidden, but the truth was there in every syllable and she could not take them back.

'Lord.' His pupils flared and the mask he wore so tightly seemed to shatter as his mouth came down upon her own.

Lionel's kisses had always been damp, weak things, lacking in ardour. But Phillip Moreland's lips held the full onslaught of the sensual, his hands in her hair turning her to the kiss, deepening and exploring. She opened to him as she never had to her husband or to the one disappointing lover she had taken after Lionel's death, and the room spun, fantasy hovering within passion, his strength and beauty both glorious and shocking. Tipping her head, she opened her mouth wider, allowing him to taste her, to know her, to seize all that he wanted, and when she cried out in a voice she hadn't heard herself use before, the voice of a want so desperate, there was no tempering it.

And take he did, with his lips and his tongue and the strength of his hands until roiling waves of desire boiled upwards and beached between them, waves she enjoyed without shame or question.

A fully clothed triumph. A startling discovery. Nothing unhidden. Warm against cold. Soft against hard. Delight amidst wonder. There was no answer to the question of what this was. There was only feeling, the candlelight flickering and the wind outside.

When he finally brought her against him and held her still she felt the rapid beat of his heart matching her own and was pleased he did not whisper untrue things, for this was enough and she could not have borne lies.

Her whole world had been turned upside down and what risks she might have believed in at the beginning of the night were nowhere near as certain now.

No future. No permanency. No ties.

A simple connection and then a severance. Just this moment. When he raised his head so that he might see the time on the long-case clock in the corner she knew that she had lost him. The kitchen was no place to be caught together, for the scullery maids would be up early.

She felt drained, her dressing gown loose and her hair tangled.

'I need to go.' She would get in first before he said it.

His glance swivelled around to her own, intense and forceful, but he did not move.

'We cannot be found here.' Her words hinted at other things.

He stepped away then, his shirt pale in the moonlight and his hair dark. She felt him there still on her body in the places that were different.

And then she left, quietly through the kitchen and up the staircase, each footfall taken as though she were walking through mud. In her room she shut the door and leaned against it, an emptiness inside.

The eighth Earl of Elmsworth, Phillip Moreland, was not for her. They had stolen a fine measure of passion but now it was finished, banished to memory. To the impossible.

Tomorrow she would leave the estate and she might never see him again. Even if they did meet at some Society event he would ignore her because he should. What had happened tonight was completely untenable, a small, forbidden connection in the long and complicated road of life.

Yet her body felt alive in a way it never had and the memory of those years lying with her husband whilst he completed his marital duty was suddenly horrifying. She had thought that was what intimacy was. A necessity. A thing to be endured. But now she knew the wonder in it, the delight and the enchantment. Phillip Moreland had shown her that at the grand old age of thirty and she would have to live with this knowledge for the rest of her life. Alone.

He loved his wife. Gretel. He had whispered her name as he'd held her and she understood from his tone how much he missed her.

Swallowing, she shook her head. She would survive this because she had survived everything else and for years and years and years. She had independence now and the ability to live well. This would not beat her and she would not relegate their kisses to a mistake either. She had wanted him and he had wanted her and they had hurt nobody at all. It was their secret to do with as they wished and one day she would look back and think that this was one of her most remarkable moments.

He had whispered Gretel's name as he'd held her. Hell, he hoped Wilhelmina St Claire had not heard that. He had whispered his wife's name to stop himself dissolving into a person he didn't recognise and it had not worked. He had been caught in the pleasure and thrill of a kiss that was unlike any other he had known. She had been selfless and daring and giving. She had kissed him with the honesty of a woman who held nothing back.

He would have kept going too, but the clock had stopped him, its hands turning to the hour of three and the possibility of those who saw to the running of the Elmsworth kitchens not far from awakening.

He sat back against the hardness of the table-top, and was glad for the reminder of discomfort.

Mrs St Claire would be gone tomorrow, gone to London and away from Hampshire. Phillip resolved to be far from the house when she went, out on one of the horses stabled here, riding on the hills above the estate so that he might watch her leave, at a safe distance.

He was not looking for another wife and besides, she had told him she had no want at all for a husband. She was undeniably pleased to be a free woman and one who was financially independent to boot, and if she waded occasionally into the sensual with others from time to time then that was her choice.

But not his. He felt as if Gretel watched him closely from her realm in the afterlife, not in some malevolent form but in the way of one who was sorry. Sorry for the weaknesses and the mistakes and for the sad times, too, when the dreams of a child conceived together had begun to slip further and further away until the illness had staked its claim.

A flirtation was not for him, no matter how tempting or sweet. He was too old for it, for one thing, and too exhausted by all that had happened for another. A simple, quiet life with easily defined boundaries and no risk at all was preferable after the years in chaos. No surprises, no broken dreams or hearts, no feelings of failure or loss that sent him to the place his mother had always said he would linger in.

He needed peace to heal and to make him stronger. His fingers shook in his lap and he cursed the inherited affliction.

Chapter Two

Eight days later Phillip journeyed across to Nettleford Park to see his brother. The house Oliver had bought was large and rambling, the gardens full of flowers and shrubs and all carefully tended.

A family home. It felt strange coming to see his younger brother, who now had a wife and three children. His own life had stopped whilst Oliver's had carried on at a faster and faster rate, until Oliver's world looked like a full and complete one.

A part of him had not wanted to come today, given the history between them, but the Elmsworth land and titles would need heirs that he had no want to provide and Oliver's progeny would take the family name and properties down through this century and on into the next one.

A red rosebush at the side of the driveway caught his attention, reminding him for some reason of Wilhelmina St Claire with its bold honesty and beauty.

He wondered how she fared in London? He had weighed up the notion of sending her a letter after she had left but had decided against it. He'd watched her go from the hills to one side of the house, a line of oaks keeping him and his horse hidden. She'd been wearing a dark green cloak, the hood rimmed in white fur, and she had stopped at the top step of the carriage and carefully looked back across the façade of Elmsworth.

A shout caught his attention and Oliver was there coming down the front steps of Nettleford Park, questions on his face.

'My God. Phillip? It is you?'

The brother he had left more than four years prior was much changed. He looked younger and freer. Phillip wondered what Oliver must be thinking of him, this tight, sad man who had returned without his wife and who was now marooned at the practically empty and isolated family estate.

'I have been wondering when you would return, Phillip. We have not had a letter in years, and to see you here now, right in front of me… Well, it is a surprise, I can tell you that.'

'I should have sent word.'

Oliver cut him off.

'No, you did not have to. Will you stay?' He looked around for luggage even as Phillip shook his head.

'I have things to do at Elmsworth that cannot be left.'

Inside he tried to think of even one task that he had to do but couldn't, the manager Oliver had employed leaving him largely redundant on his own land.

He wished he had not returned to England at all. He wished he were still in the Americas, on the road, travelling, close to no one, lost in the many miles of a new and seemingly endless continent.

A woman was walking quickly towards them now, holding a very small baby, a beautiful blonde woman with deep dimples in each cheek and eyes of a colour he had never seen before on anyone: emerald, like the sea in some tropical cove with white sands running beneath it to amplify the hue.

'We have been waiting for you to come, my lord, for Oliver was certain at Christmas that it would be this year, and here you are, like magic and conjured up before us.'

'Phillip, meet my wife, Esther, and our youngest child. James was born only a month ago and we have two other little ones who you will no doubt meet the moment we step inside the house.'

'You are one of the Barrington-Halls, are you not? I can see the family likeness.'

'I am. My aunt and uncle are Lord and Lady Duggan.'

'I always thought that they were good people.'

She nodded. 'We were very sorry to hear the news of your wife, my lord. I lost my mother when I was young and there is nothing anyone can say to take away the pain of a loved one gone, but be assured I do understand at least a part of it.'

'Thank you.' He liked her honesty. So many people had skirted around Gretel's death and barely mentioned it. Certainly they did not quantify loss with pain as Oliver's wife did or hold his hand tightly as if her warmth might imbue a little hope into the coldness that was so much a part of him now.

His brother said nothing but he could see the question on his face. They would want something more about his wife's passing.

'Gretel died in her mother's arms.'

'A peaceful death, then.' Esther's words were soft.

Wilhelmina St Claire had said the very same thing but today he allowed his brother and sister-in-law the illusion of it. He wondered why he had not done the same with her in the dark kitchen of Elmsworth.

My God, the woman was creeping into his thoughts more and more and it had to stop. He was pleased when they began to walk towards the house.

'I'd heard on the grapevine that there had been

guests at the estate but nothing was said of you being home.' His brother said this with the reserve which was so much part of their relationship now.

'You speak, I think, of the visitors last week? Mrs St Claire and her travelling companions, the elderly McAllistair sisters, stayed one night at Elmsworth as Mrs St Claire had been violently ill from eating food at an inn and could not continue on with her journey to London.'

'Mrs Wilhelmina St Claire?' Esther said this with surprise.

He nodded.

'Is she not the most fascinating woman? Every man she ever meets falls at her feet in adoration and yet she does not give an impression of interest in any of them. Did you know she was a widow, my lord?'

'Phillip. Yes, I had heard that.'

'Her husband was a leading light in the art of astronomy and was wealthy enough to build a telescope of such proportion it could be used to watch the stars. He discovered quite a few, I think, and named one after her.'

'So you know her well?'

'We are acquainted but I would not say I know her well as Oliver and I are so rarely in London these days. I admire her though for she is a rare woman who is both kind and clever and her opinions are well regarded in Society.'

They'd walked up the steps now and into a large room with flowers everywhere.

'From the garden Esther insists on tending herself,' Oliver explained, and Phillip could hear both pride and love in the words. His brother was different now, happier, more open. He was amazed at the transformation four years could have on a person, and thought of his own lack of joy.

He had never been particularly happy. He had loved Gretel to the height of his ability but, looking at Esther and Oliver, he suddenly wondered if that had been too little.

Gretel had said as much to him as she had lain dying. She'd said she wished they had met when they were both older and wiser. She had also said that love had many shades and that maybe theirs had been blighted by the problems in their past.

The world tipped slightly and he placed his hand on the nearest wall.

'Are you well?' Oliver moved towards him, but the moment of dizziness was gone and Phillip smiled, feeling more himself.

'I think the sea voyage took more out of me than I realised,' he gave back, knowing that it was not the case at all. It was just that he wanted to return to Elmsworth, to its silence and its familiarity. He wanted to sit in the quiet of his library with a cognac in his hand and be alone with his ghosts and his sorrows and his what-might-have-beens.

But the next second a tumbling boy child hurtled down the stairs, a fraught-looking woman behind telling him to slow down and remember his manners. Behind her came another servant with a younger girl in her arms.

'Papa, Papa.' The little boy tugged at Oliver's trousers. 'Is he your brother? He looks like you.'

'William, say hello to your Uncle Phillip, who has come all the way from America to Hampshire.'

'Today?'

Esther and Oliver both laughed. 'No, my darling,' Esther said and kneeled down to him. 'Remember we told you that America was a long way from England and you had to travel weeks and weeks on a ship to get there?'

William looked at Phillip with eyes the same shade as his mother's.

The little girl then held out a well-chewed doll. 'Molly.'

This child had black hair and blue eyes, the stamp of the Morelands so easily upon her it made Phillip take in a breath. Life went on binding those who had been with those who were next to come. A bridge to the future. There was something so right about it that it made him relax as he reached out for the small, flaxen-haired doll.

'Well, hello, Molly. Your hair is very long.'

The child laughed.

'Juliette must trust you if she's offering up her favourite doll.' Oliver said this with humour.

'Would it be rude to give it back now?' The wetness of the chewed clothes was faintly worrying.

'Not at all. Our daughter would most likely begin to cry if you did not. She seldom lets Molly out of her hands.'

Just as his brother had said, the child cuddled the doll fiercely on its return and in that moment Phillip had an aching want to know what it must feel like to be a father, to have little ones with all their unique ways depending on you and loving you.

He saw Esther looking at him strangely, as if perhaps she had guessed his thoughts.

'Children never allow one much time for introspection,' she stated then and he nodded, thinking that would be one of the main reasons he would most like to have them.

Half an hour later he was relieved to have gained some time with Oliver though, left alone with his brother, he was acutely aware of the awkward silence between them.

'How are you, Phillip?' Oliver's question came as he sat down.

'I have been busy with the estate and readying myself for a trip to London.'

'Are you going for business?'

'Not completely.' When he said no more, Oliver smiled.

'You were always far more secretive than I was. Sometimes I wondered after our childhood if you ever told anyone anything.'

'I was married.'

'Your wife always gave me the impression of a woman who was hard to fathom. She was certainly… mercurial.'

Oliver stood and crossed over to the drinks cabinet. Pouring two generous whiskies, he came back and sat down, offering one to Phillip.

'You are referring to Gretel's desperation to have a child?'

'I am. We never talked about anything after you shot me.'

'That was because I didn't believe your side of the story at the time.'

'But now you do?'

'Imminent death brings on a will to undo tangled mistakes. Gretel told me what had happened between you both in the weeks before she passed away.

She said she had gone unbidden to your townhouse and left when you refused outright her offer of sex so that she might conceive an heir for Elmsworth.'

'A complete reversal of her lie at the time that held me at fault of attacking her physically?'

'Exactly.'

'Well, I am at least grateful that she told you the truth and I am sorry that it has taken so long for us to speak about it.'

Raising his left hand, Phillip allowed Oliver to see the shake in it. 'If it's any consolation at all, when I confronted you I did mean to miss.'

'I know. After our childhood there is a certain glue that can never be unstuck.'

'The glue of surviving catastrophe?'

Oliver nodded.

'You seem to have done that well in the years since I have been away from England.'

'My wife saved me, from fury and from fracture and from the bloody curse of the Morelands.'

Taking a breath, Phillip looked directly at him. 'Then you are lucky.'

Phillip limited himself to one glass of cognac that evening after arriving home because he knew he had been drinking too heavily. This was his second bottle in less than ten days and the comfort it had given him a week ago was no longer there.

He had stayed only a little while longer at his brother's estate after their conversation but he was glad he had spoken with Oliver for there was so much hidden in them both, the regret and anger and lies only just holding back chaos after their brutal childhood.

He wouldn't go back to Nettleford Park until he could sort his feelings out, his envy and his resentment. Poor emotions that he was ashamed of but there it was. Oliver's life had turned a corner whilst his was plummeting downhill at an alarming rate.

A letter propped on the mantel then caught his attention, for it had not been there when he'd left in the morning. Standing up, he walked over and plucked it from its position. A London postcode, the red wax at the back stamped with the letter W. His finger traced over the indent and then he opened it.

Dear Lord Elmsworth,
I realise it to be most remiss of me not to have sent you a note immediately after I arrived back in London to say thank you for your generosity in accommodating our party at a difficult time.

If you are in London in the near future, I would like to be able to pay back a little of your hospitality in person.
Yours sincerely,
Mrs Wilhelmina St Claire

Phillip read it three times before putting it down on the table in front of him and then he read it for a fourth time. Her address was written along the bottom of the page.

It was a confounding message. Did 'I would like to be able to pay back a little of your hospitality in person' have connotations that suggested something else?

Raking both hands through his hair, he leaned back. Or was this simply a note of thanks that any well-mannered person might send to an acquaintance who had done them an unexpected favour?

Changing position, he took another sip of cognac and looked at the words again. Probably the second option, if he was honest. Bringing the paper to his nose, he sniffed.

Only ink and parchment. No smell at all of gardenias.

His glance then went to the picture on the opposite side of the room, a portrait of himself and Gretel done years ago now. When they were both young and hopeful. Before life had touched them with all the tumbling betrayals.

'I am sorry,' he whispered, though in all truth he did not know what he had to apologise for.

Turning the note over, he looked at the same handwriting on the front of the missive. He could feel

Mrs St Claire here before him and remembered the warmth and the welcome of her mouth. Shaking his head, he closed his eyes, recalling the cleft in her chin, her golden glance, her teasing words, her sensuality.

He wanted to screw the parchment up and throw it away, throw away these feelings which could only cause harm. He needed to recall the distance and the pride he was famous for and remember his mother's words in the last letter she had left him saying that he was destined to melancholy. Like her.

Gretel had felt it and told him so too, she who had been marked with her own sadness. Together they had floundered, until the sickness had come and made everything else unimportant. In the last year together when their time was running out they had found more happiness than in all the preceding ones and he was glad of it.

He lifted his glass up to toast her, the beautiful young Gretel Carmichael as he had first seen her, walking in a white gown down the main staircase of the Westinghouse ballroom, but he wished the portrait were not there, in his library, intruding in the one room that he felt was his.

Past and present and future. All three were here, perfectly balanced in this moment of time, and Phillip wondered which way he might turn. Back into memories or forward to life?

Grasping the letter, he held it tight and thought if it was not a solution it was at least a direction. He capped the cognac and replaced the bottle in the cabinet before walking to the window to watch the early darkness of the night sky. Tonight the clouds had rolled back and a million stars twinkled down at him.

Out of the blue he wondered which star Mr Lionel St Claire had discovered and named after his wife. The brightest one, he imagined as his glance fastened on a star low on the eastern horizon.

Needing to calm these thoughts, Phillip then walked upstairs to the second floor, stopping in the suite of rooms where he guessed Mrs Wilhelmina St Claire must have slept on her one night here.

The older ladies would have been grouped together in the larger room, but the smaller alcove overlooking the front of the house perhaps had been hers. He tried to see it through her eyes: the floral wallpaper, the row of books on a shelf near the window, a carpet that was thick and warm under her feet.

A good choice with the view reaching down to the lake. Had there been a moon that night? He could not remember but hoped there had been as it would have been visible across the soft folds of the countryside to the east.

All the landmarks that he recognised. Nothing foreign or unfamiliar. He knew the trees and the smell of the seasons, he understood the patterns of rain and wind and snow, the soft heat in summer and the colour of the changing leaves in autumn.

My place.

In place.

Home.

It had been so long since he had felt such a belonging.

The silence he'd often hated here was replaced by known sounds, comforting in the way they belonged to no one time, no one person, no one truth. They were here before him and they would be here after. The flow of nature and time and earth. It made one's problems seem smaller and less significant and allowed acceptance and relief to gather. Even the lake tonight looked silver and calm, all of its uneasy black depths hidden.

The conversation with Oliver today had allowed an easing, though, a way of understanding his wife's actions and Oliver's too. They had all been caught in a tangled web that was now loosening, and communication would allow him a way of moving on from the guilt that always overshadowed any thought of his brother.

He needed a change. He needed to step out of anger, sadness and shame. Looking at the lines on his left hand, he hoped that whatever came next would allow him the strength to live well and with honour.

Chapter Three

The Wilsons' ball in Mayfair in the second week of June was a huge affair, the rooms decorated in dark green so that the whole place gave the effect of an enchanted forest. Great fragrant boughs of pine had been placed in every corner of the adjoining salons to add to the illusion.

Willa, by chance, had on a dress of mid-green, a flouncy number that she was not all that keen on but felt the need to wear a few times at least in order to justify its expense. She smiled at such a thought now that she was moderately wealthy, but old habits were hard to break and her mother's parsimonious ways were difficult to simply ignore even though she had been dead for nigh on eight years.

She had pinned her hair up tonight, eschewing the more feminine style of the moment, and the earrings she wore were her very favourite, long pearl drops with stones of amber at each end. The feathers she had attached to her cap were probably a bit much but she had long since disposed with the worry of fashion and had liked the way the colour in them matched the amber.

A good friend, Miss Anna Cherton, joined her before she had gone ten yards.

'You look like a rare bird of prey, Willa. I love the way your maid has done your hair.'

Willa waved her hand. 'Oh, no, this is my doing. If I left things to Hetty I would have a veritable waterfall of ringlets falling on each side and a pink silk rose tucked into the top of it.'

'Like Miss Violet Broome?' Anna returned and they both watched as the youngest daughter of Lord Broome crossed the room before them.

'Well, she looks attractive in anything, really.' Willa seldom said things that could be construed as criticism, and besides, the girl was young and rather sweet.

For a moment she felt as old as she had ever felt, her thirty-first birthday in a few months feeling suddenly close. Perhaps she should have dressed with a little less oddness and followed the fashions in the way every other female in the room seemed wont to do.

'Did the final viewing of Belton Park go well?'

'It did. The lawyers only have to complete the documents and then they can all be signed.'

'Will you be sad never to go there again?'

'Not at all. In fact, the truth is it will be a relief to have it off my hands.'

Anna threaded their fingers together. 'I was speaking with the middle McAllistair sister the other day and she said you had been laid low with a stomach ailment on your way back to London. She commented on the Elmsworth estate with a particular tone.'

The mention of the place in which she had taken shelter jolted Willa. She had thought of the Earl's kisses every night since they had happened and could not make any sense of her reaction.

George Fitzgibbon and Freddie Boucher had now come over to join them, two men whom Willa had known ever since moving to the city.

'Did I hear you mentioning the Elmsworth estate, Anna? Then you must know that the eighth Earl has finally returned to these shores. Word has it he is installed in Hampshire after the loss of his beautiful wife in the Americas, though as yet he has not ventured across to the city.'

'My goodness, it's been years since he left England, hasn't it?' Anna asked this and Freddie was quick to supply an answer.

'At least four. The family was odd, a fractured family who seemed to be both melancholic and arrogant, if such a mix is possible.'

'Yet Lord Phillip Moreland was more than handsome, Freddie, for I remember him vividly. He was a man who had the hearts of the female gender fluttering everywhere but he chose Miss Gretel Carmichael before either of them was even twenty and married her within a few weeks, much to the chagrin of all the girls and women left.'

Willa was interested in this titbit from Anna. She herself was just seventeen when she had said 'I do' in the small church at Belton with her parents and a few of Lionel's friends present as witnesses.

'The Society wedding of that year, it is said.' This came from George. 'My oldest brother was sure every man in London was half in love with Gretel Carmichael, with her classical looks and pale hair, but Moreland was leaving nothing to chance and popped the question before anyone else could. And then they disappeared into the wilds of Hampshire, returning to London only for a month of each season before going back.'

'A love story,' Anna sighed. 'A wonderful tale of two people meeting who were destined to be together right until death parted them, a state of affairs that completely broke his heart.'

Willa looked away, a faint niggle of shame inside her which was difficult to banish. Did ruined people like her have a propensity to tarnish those who were unsullied? She had never loved Lionel right from the beginning and had given up trying to in the first few months, much to her mother's dismay.

Gretel Carmichael, on the other hand, had loved her husband well and properly and had led a happy and unblemished life.

Lionel's anger and her own were the very opposite, the discord of hate and fear. When he had fallen down and down until there was nothing of life left in him, the angels of freedom had danced around her in utter relief.

She pulled herself back into the moment, clamping her teeth together and trying to smile, the shock of memory leaving her chilled here in the laughter and noise of an enchanted woodland ballroom.

As the musicians at one end of the room began to play George Fitzgibbon held out his hand and, needing the distraction from Anna's words, she went into his arms for a waltz. She had known him ever since she had arrived in London and he had pursued her from the first moment they'd met. A man who liked grand gestures and great emotion and one whom she had never encouraged in any way, save in friendship.

The music of the flute rose high above the violins,

the scent of flowers pinned amongst the greenery and candles infused with lavender oil. This was her life now, independent and strong. She was a lot different from the woman she had once been, a young woman beholden to her husband and to her parents and isolated essentially from all others in their efforts to control her.

'Marry me, Willa, and we can leave for the Americas in the spring.' Horror ran through her at his words.

'If I did not know you better, George, I might almost think you meant it.'

'Perhaps, my love, I do. My mother and father are insistent on a bride before the end of the year and I cannot think of a girl I could do better with.'

'A girl is something I hardly am, George.'

'A woman, then, a beautiful and interesting woman.'

She shook her head. 'Miss Leonora Blanchard over there is the female you should pursue. She is both kind and clever and I have it on good account that she is an avid reader. Like you.'

'She is young.'

'You are not yet twenty-seven.'

'So you are refusing me?'

'I am indeed but only because I know I would shatter your heart if I had the temerity to accept.'

'I met your husband once. Did you know that?'

Left speechless at his admission, Willa waited to see what he might say next.

'I remember Mr Lionel St Claire as a stern, upright man of strong opinion.'

'That is a reasonable description.'

'I could not see him enjoying a London salon with discourse that edges on radical debate.'

'I agree. My late husband would have struggled in this company.'

'Struggled as you did perhaps in his estate of silence and rule?'

Willa kept smiling because it did not pay to let too much out to a man like George, as he had a memory that stored everything.

'How long have we known each other, George?'

'A little over two years, Wilhelmina. I met you on the first night you arrived in London. I remember it like it was yesterday.'

'One loyal friend is worth ten thousand relatives.' She uttered this with a smile on her face.

'Euripides?'

'One well-read and loyal friend,' she amended and allowed him to lead her into a practised and graceful swirl. Why did men always have to ruin friendship by imagining more? Why could they not be happy with less? She hoped George might understand that after her refusal to take his offer seriously he should not make it again, though when his hand squeezed her own in a deliberate way she thought she might not be so lucky.

'Lord Phillip Moreland, the Eighth Earl of Elmsworth.'

The name rang across the room just as the dance ended and the entire salon looked up at the grand staircase to one end. He was alone, dressed in black, a tall, dark-haired man with an air of aristocracy so easily discernible even from this distance.

'Well, well. The lost Earl is here tonight and we can watch the Society mamas descend on him. It will be fascinating.' Anna's words were whispered as she and Freddie rejoined them, but all around the room similar sentiments were being expressed. Willa could only stand still and observe him, her heart beating fast and her teeth tightly clenched together.

If Phillip Moreland heard the gossip he gave an excellent impression of having no care at all for it as he moved forward to be surrounded by people wanting to speak with him.

Here, he was different, his place in Society cemented perhaps by his recent loss and his long absence. He looked in control too, smiling politely at all those who surged to be near him.

The air all around her was colder, the ease of the

night sliding into fear. Would he see her? Would he say something or would he ignore her entirely?

He looked like the veritable definition of a high and mighty lord and one with whom she had nothing in common at all.

Reaching out for a fluted glass of champagne from a passing servant, she drank it quickly, needing the fortification to relax her and enable a smile. She would leave as soon as she was able to go without comment, and next time she saw him she would be able to manage a lot better.

Phillip remembered all the things he had hated about London Society as he came down the stairs. The gossip. The expectations. The matrons who eyed him as a prize for their daughters. Gretel had largely protected him from it all when he was here last but with her gone… He was engulfed by the crowd that swelled around him as he reached the bottom step.

The invitation to the Wilsons' ball had come unexpectedly and he'd felt it was probably time to make some sort of an effort to participate again in the world he'd been born to. Still, this whole journey into London seemed misguided and he wished he'd stayed in Hampshire, away from it all.

Tobias Wilson, the Earl of Hammond, was suddenly there, his sister beside him.

'It is good to see you again, Elmsworth, though I was sorry to hear the news of your wife.'

'Thank you.'

'But we are very honoured that you decided to grace our ball as your first outing back in Society.'

Phillip smiled, not because the thought pleased him but because it was expected. The prodigal son coming home, so to speak, after a long time in the wilderness.

'And things have changed in your absence, although by all accounts it seems you have returned to an estate that has prospered without you.'

'My brother's good choices. The manager Oliver put in place at Elmsworth is more than competent.'

'A fortunate happenstance, then, for others have not been anywhere near as lucky when they have forsaken all responsibility and ventured elsewhere.'

The sentiment was loud and clear and Phillip remembered why he had never been that fond of Tobias Wilson. He'd been a jealous, difficult youth and had grown into the same sort of man.

His sister, Miss Clementine Wilson, placed her hand on his sleeve.

'There has been much talk about when you would appear in London for the season, Lord Elmsworth. We all knew you were finally back, of course, but no one had seen you. Are you planning on staying in the city for long?'

'Just a few days. I have some business with my lawyer to attend to and after that I will return to Hampshire.'

A servant bearing a tray approached them and he took a glass of champagne. He needed fortification in a room such as this and gratefully took a sip.

'It is French,' Clementine said. 'My brother has it brought over especially.'

'Then he has good taste in fine wines. From memory, the Hammonds had some interests in the vineyards of northwestern France. I am presuming they still have them.'

Tobias had rejoined their conversation and began to laugh. 'You were always surprising people at school with your recall, Phillip. Do you remember that card game we used to play, the one where you had to match the images, and you always came out on top? Benjamin Harcourt thought you had marked the cards until he got hold of another pack and you beat us all just as convincingly. God, those were the days, were they not, when we were young and free and the world was at our feet, no problems anywhere in sight? Benjamin is here tonight somewhere, though God knows how long he will stay, for he is known for leaving every social event as early as he is able to and creeping back to Richmond.'

Interested, Phillip looked around in an attempt at locating his old friend, and frowned as he saw Mrs Wilhelmina St Claire on the other side of the room, a strange feathered cap on her head and a gown a few shades lighter than the green on the salon walls. The group around her were animated and she was reaching now for a glass of the same champagne he'd just been commenting on.

When her eyes caught his she looked away first, colour washing into her cheeks, her jaw held tight and her fingers grasping the fluted glass with fervour.

He knew instantly that she was horrified to see him there and that thought brought him sorrow, though he could not fathom as to why it should. Perhaps it was because she had been the first person in a long time that he had been truthful with, a woman with whom he had shared a few hours in the middle of a lonely night without interruption or expectation.

The man beside her watched her closely. Lord George Fitzgibbon. He recognised the fellow as the youngest sibling of one of his Eton classmates. But when gloved fingers were placed on his sleeve Phillip looked away. Lady Leggett beamed at him, a wide smile on her face.

'Lord Elmsworth, it is so good to have you back in England. Have you seen your brother yet?'

He remembered that she and Oliver had once been a pair.

'Oliver and his wife live near me now in Hampshire and their brood of children is increasing with each and every year.'

Leave her with no question as to Oliver's situation, he thought, somewhat disconcerted when she laughed.

'Esther is a friend of mine, my lord, and I am frequently a visitor at Nettleford Park. I also know your brother has been wondering when you would come home for years, for he often mentions you.'

A different reply than he might have expected. The knowledge that the world here had changed remarkably since he and Gretel had boarded the ship to the Americas left him on edge. It had been four years ago he'd left England for what was supposed to be only a year to escort his sick wife home to her parents in Virginia. But Gretel's death had left him questioning everything and he'd taken to the road to try and sort himself out. Oliver's competent stewardship of the Elmsworth estate had allowed him time to come to terms with a return to his old life here but finally he could no longer expect others to do a job he was born to.

'Would you dance with me, my lord? It is a waltz.'

He could not refuse without sounding churlish and so he took her offered hand and walked towards the floor. Mrs St Claire was closer here; he could see her green dress out of the corner of his eye, though he made an effort not to look directly at her.

The next problem hadn't occurred to him. Winifred Leggett was a spectacular dancer and he could barely remember the steps but she was also kind in her tutelage and kept him to the rhythm.

'It's been a while…' he began but she did not let him finish.

'It's like riding a bicycle, I expect. One only needs to practise.'

Suddenly he perceived she might not only be talking about the dance and when her fingers stroked his own he knew that she wasn't.

Phillip Moreland was dancing with Lady Winifred Leggett. He looked a bit lost in the intricacies of the steps but his partner was an accomplished dancer and was dragging him through it with aplomb, her laughter heard from where she stood a good ten yards away.

They suited each other, Willa thought, both wealthy

and beautiful, attributes that were highly valued within the narrow confines of the Ton.

He looked happier in this setting, the adulation and regard from others around him so discernible that even the trials of his personal tragedies were somewhat diminished.

She was glad of it, for him.

She'd caught his glance before but he had not looked her way since, the green dress probably as much of a mistake as the outlandish feathers in her headpiece. She seldom thought of her clothing in such a way and admonished herself for the pettiness as George's laughter brought her back to the moment.

'One wonders how Elmsworth so easily commands a room, given his lengthy absences and his family circumstance.'

'What circumstance?' She could not help but ask this.

'His mother went mad and it was thought before he left England that he would follow her into such a state.'

'Why? He hardly looks deranged to me.'

'The rumour is Phillip Moreland tried to kill his brother after some sort of a fight between them.' This titbit was whispered so that the others might not hear, and shock ran through her.

'My goodness. Is this common knowledge?'

'My older brother was a close friend of Oliver Moreland's but no one in either circle spoke a word about it, so in truth who knows the full story because no charges were ever laid? It's just you seem interested in the Earl somehow and I don't want you hurt.'

The old protections kicked in quickly and Willa laughed, hearing in the sound everything that she wanted him to. 'Your imagination is misguided. Come, let me introduce you to the lovely Miss Blanchard.'

An hour later Willa was standing alone on one side of the room, having just finished a lengthy and exhausting quadrille with the elderly Lord Hamilton, a man whose company she had always enjoyed because he spoke so kindly of his family as he related all their various amusing escapades.

Anna joined her, frowning. 'I think that dance gets longer each time I complete it, and Lord Bambrook was hardly an easy partner.'

They both watched Nigel Bambrook threading his way back towards them with a tray of full glasses.

'At least he is reliable,' Willa replied, 'and I'm so thirsty I could do with a drink. Besides, he often looks a little lost in these busy Society settings.'

'I'm not as generous as you are, Willa. Give me

the Earl of Elmsworth any day, a man who looks neither amenable nor kind but is devilishly attractive in that dangerous sort of way that all the ladies love.'

Wilhelmina had to smile. 'Lord Moreland is by all accounts still deeply saddened about his wife's passing. I do not think he is in the market for another relationship, no matter how tempting the bait.'

'You think I am tempting?'

'Of course you are.'

She enjoyed hearing Anna laugh as Bambrook rejoined them, fussing about whose drink was whose.

'You are a shining knight, my lord,' Willa stated, grateful for their more secluded position to one side of a pillar. Being out of the way suited her, for she had not caught sight of Phillip Moreland for a good half an hour, though the noise from the other salon alerted her to the fact that he was probably in the big group of men and women enjoying the ball there. She should have left to find her carriage but she could not quite do it, the churning excitement in her stomach from just knowing he was close keeping her at the ball. She knew it was foolishness to feel this way, given her history, but there it was and there was no way to change it. She drank the glass of champagne with haste and hoped it might dull the ache inside.

The first sounds of the music from the orchestra

were again beginning to fill the room as strings were tuned in preparation for the next brace of dances when Anna's surprised expression distracted her.

'My goodness, could Lord Elmsworth possibly be coming towards us?'

Turning, Willa saw the Earl not five yards away, the darkness of his clothes emphasising the tan on his skin, his blue eyes fixed upon her.

'Mrs St Claire.'

'My lord.'

The silence stretched between them, her surroundings falling away, so that it seemed it was only them in the room, the rest of Society disappearing into shadow.

'I came to ask you for the next dance, if indeed you do have it free?'

Unable to decline, she placed her hand on his arm as he led her through a throng of people, all reappearing now in colour, noise and movement. Such a juxtaposition was dizzying.

'I got your note thanking me for my hospitality at Elmsworth.' His voice was quiet, one hand around hers and the other at her waist as they faced one another.

'I did not expect to see you here, my lord.' It was all she could give him back, her heart beating so violently she thought if he let her go she might fall.

'I have heard that exact same sentiment all night from everyone I have talked to.'

The words between them were formal and ordinary, far from their conversation in his kitchen with her dressed only in her night attire and her hair loose.

He sounded slightly bored, as if all this socialising was only to be got through. Irritation gave her own words an edge. 'The conjecture, my lord, is because Society in general has so little to be surprised by.'

He looked at her directly now, his blue eyes sharpening. 'Then perhaps my role tonight is to give others a small rest from such perpetual tedium?'

At this she did laugh and she felt the knots in her stomach begin to loosen. He was not different. He was exactly the same, his words affecting her here as they had done in the night-time kitchen of Elmsworth Manor.

'A worthy aspiration.'

'I thought you might see it as such.'

She could feel the breath of his words against her cheek.

'I imagine after such a long time away in another land England feels somewhat different, my lord.' She was starting to find her feet again, his manner giving her cues back to normalcy, the relief of it all a reprieve.

'Indeed, it does. The formality here is something I'd forgotten about.'

She nodded. 'I understand what you mean exactly. When I arrived in London I was newly widowed and out of my depth with Society here. It was a difficult time.'

'You do not look uncertain now.'

'London's diversity doesn't allow one to hide away.'

'Which is probably a good thing,' he returned. 'It has been a long while since I have been out in this city.'

'And so much has changed, I should imagine.'

'Perhaps,' he said softly as he gazed around the room. 'But so much has not.'

'You did not enjoy London, my lord? Before, I mean.' She wondered if the question was too personal even as she asked it, but he took no umbrage.

'Expectations can be wearying and here they arrive in many forms. The ball. The dances. The conversations. But I am beginning to feel more established in Hampshire.'

'In your role there? In the running of a large estate?'

'I forgot how many questions you ask.'

Willa hated the blush that came across her cheeks.

'I did not mean that as a criticism, Mrs St Claire.

Sometimes questions are a good thing because they can bring about a change.'

'You sound like your brother.'

This time he laughed. 'Esther mentioned that she was acquainted with you when I visited Nettleford on my arrival. Oliver looked happier than I have ever seen him.'

'Because he has found a nest with Esther and the children.'

'A nest?'

'Most men need these to flourish.'

'Is this a scientific fact?'

'No. My parents would be horrified by such a deduction. I told you they were scientists, did I not? It's more of an observation, I think, but the nest has to be a happy one or the whole theory falls apart.'

'Do you have many of these theories, Mrs St Claire?'

'I think I do, my lord. I think a lifetime of watching people forms the sort of knowledge in one that is undeniable.'

'I have heard you enjoy evenings of discussion at your house. Are these the sort of things spoken of?'

'Oh, there are no rules. You say what you wish to and receive back an opinion. No one is right or wrong unless they are derogatory and mean-minded.'

'In which case they are thrown out?'

'No, not even that. We try to reform even the bleakest of bigots.'

'Who is "we"?'

She smiled. 'Probably just me. I find if a meeting is run in kindness it is generally successful.'

'When is the next one?'

Surprise made her frown. 'You are thinking of coming?'

'Am I not allowed?'

'Of course you are; it is just…these discussions are open to everyone and as such they have a certain flavour…'

'The flavour of democracy?'

His humour was wry. 'On second thoughts, I think you would do very well as an attendee, my lord, and I will send you an invitation.'

All around them people watched, interested eyes noting their every move, and Willa understood for a moment how exhausting it must be for him. There could be no false steps or inadvisable actions without repercussion. Even now Willa imagined her name might be bandied around tomorrow in surprise as an unsuitable partner for an earl who needed to be married and providing heirs for the wealthy and flourishing estate of Elmsworth.

George Fitzgibbon to one side caught her eye, his frown heavy, and Anna at the other end of the room looked only astonished. Another moment out of time that simply could not last.

'You are a far better dancer than me, Mrs St Claire.'

'Which is a wonder because for years I had no practice at all.'

'Until you came to London?'

'There are things here that I have found lovely.'

'Such as?'

'The libraries. The architecture. The ideas.'

'You are a bluestocking?' His smile was beautiful.

'I am a woman catching up with a life I did not have.'

'And such freedom is beguiling?'

'More than even that, I think. It is astonishing.'

Phillip Moreland did not answer as they listened to the last strains of Brahms but he held her close before he stepped back to bow.

A simple ending like a hundred others all across the ballroom floor and then a woman was at his side, her hand resting upon his arm in a manner that suggested that they knew each other well.

'My lord. You promised me this dance.'

He turned away, an easy transition, with apparently no thoughts of staying.

'Indeed I did, Miss Hammond.' The woman's attractive voice drifted back to her as they left and, smoothing her skirts down, Willa crossed the floor and made her way to the front door.

Lord Elmsworth needed a wife and a family to bring him back to a fine life had she not just told him so? Her own nest was barren and singular and would remain that way. Any wish of more was both pointless and dangerous. Dangerous because if she let herself get attracted to a man who was plainly not for her it could only cause hurt for them both and she had had enough of that in her life.

Lifting her head, she gave thanks to the host and hostess and made her way out, pleased to settle into the gloom and the privacy of her carriage.

'Ah, Lionel,' she said softly beneath her breath as the driver called on the horses and she was homeward bound. 'Why on earth did I ever agree to marry you?'

Phillip Moreland had been attentive to her tonight but nothing more. He had behaved impeccably and formally, a grand earl returned to his rightful place into a Society that worshipped him.

She admonished herself for expecting it to be different. A foolish hope with her advancing years and her unwise history. He had probably felt sorry for her, truth be told, and perhaps regretful for the scene late at night in the Elmsworth kitchen. Part of him may have also worried about scandal and if she had spoken to anyone about their unwise encounter.

She was a woman who had made the wrong choices in life and had found peace in her quiet existence here in London. Why was it, then, that the excitement welling just from his touch was again threatening everything? She changed her position on the seat, cursing the thin flare of heat that was welling deep inside, curdling sense and making it harder to breathe.

Closing her eyes against the moving lights of London town, she leant back and let her feelings come, her soft moans bringing warmth as a release claimed her.

She could not temper the tears either that fell down her cheeks. So many years of nothing and now this everything. It was her solace and her secret.

Phillip had seen her leave, a solitary figure in green who made straight for the door at the very far end of the room. She was taller than most of the other women here and so it was easy to watch her, the chandeliers adding a lighter tinge to her dark hair.

'Mrs St Claire is certainly a woman men notice, my lord, for there is something about her that is hidden, I think, a mystery. By all accounts her husband was rather a possessive man with a temper, and when she first came down to London with him years ago she was a very quiet thing. Now I think her opinion is often sought on all types of topics, though some do say she is a little too opinionated.'

He did not wish for this gossip from Clementine Wilson and refrained from answering, even as he willed the dance to an end.

'I hope you will stay in London this Season, my lord, as my brother would be most appreciative of your company and friendship. He is often rather lonely these days. His wife, Patricia, is an unusual person and…'

Phillip simply stopped listening. This was exactly why he had largely absented himself from Society, with all the innuendo and shuttered criticism. He wished Mrs St Claire were still here so that he could have asked her for another dance and talked some more. Her conversation was interesting and different, and there was an honesty in her words that was refreshing.

He remembered the address at the foot of the letter she had sent him. Russell Square in Bloomsbury. Perhaps when he left here he would instruct his driver to pass by the house so he could at least see where it was that she lived.

A few hours later Willa brushed her hair out in front of the mirror in her bedroom. It was so much longer now than she had ever worn it, the tumbling curls almost reaching to her waist. Lionel had never liked it past her shoulders, chiding her each time he saw it down.

'Only young girls wear their hair at such a length, Wilhelmina, and you are a long way past that. Such a vanity ill suits you.'

So she had cut it time and time again to prevent argument and to curtail censure. Such a docile, obedient wife. Such an easy target, too, for a man whose own life ambitions were falling into tatters.

The heavens above had failed to release their secrets to him no matter how many hours he spent trying to decipher them, and the high hopes of unfulfilled academic attainments were a bitter pill to swallow.

As Willa pushed back the thin satin of her gown, the ugly scar on her right thigh was evident, the glass from the broken telescope having sliced deep into her flesh. Tracing the line down to her knee, she was filled with the sadness of so many wasted years and, leaning over, she pulled a journal from the bottom of her cabinet, the red leather scuffed now, and torn.

Poems and lines of prose filled the pages, each word an outlet for the much younger version of herself desperately trying to make sense of her situation. No one had helped her. Not her mother or her father. Not the doctor who had been summoned to stitch the wound. Not the priest at the church whom she had sought out for guidance. Not the housekeeper, either, who, whilst kind, had had no wish to lose her job.

No, she had made her bed and she'd had to lie down in it. Lie down with a man who'd become worse and worse with each passing year, a husband who'd used cruel words as a way of communication and anger as a method of control.

She'd thought it her fault at first that she could not please him, could not reason with him, could not still his disappointments. Then she had merely given up and accepted her lot, cleaning the house with more avid regularity and staying well out of his way.

When he had fallen down and down onto the stone terrace from the small balcony off the library she had watched with disbelief. The fluttering pages of her ripped book had gone with him, floating in a way that he had not, the dull thud of his head against the stones beneath so very un-survivable.

She'd stood there in the silence, in the space between them, the realisation of freedom present. She had then taken the gold marriage ring from her finger and thrown it as hard as she could, the symbol of oppression tumbling over and over against the blue of the sky before it was lost.

At her feet had been more torn pages that her husband had yanked out in his anger and those she'd tenderly lifted, safe in her hands as Lionel St Claire had not been, her push against him hard, too hard perhaps; she'd seen the moment his shoe had caught the jutting edge of the balcony, his attempt to grab for her, the astonishment as he had missed, the howl of blame, the curse of his marriage, a thousand moments between them sealed in this one final time as he fell, fury crystalizing in his last breath.

'YOUR FAULT.'

These words were capitalised on the back cover of her journal.

And they were true. She had pushed him away from her in order to retrieve her tattered journal. He was a big man and it was a hard push but she had never expected him to lose his footing as he had done.

Biting her lip, Willa felt the salty taste of blood.

It was foolish to expect her life in London should now slot easily into place, given her past mistakes, and it was irrational to foster any sort of relationship with a man like the aristocratic Earl of Elmsworth.

But it had been lovely tonight in the ballroom of the Wilsons to pretend and to imagine that Phillip Moreland had sought her out for the dance because he felt something for her, that he liked her, that he had enjoyed their conversations.

'Stop,' she whispered into the empty darkness and turned to make herself ready for bed.

Chapter Four

Phillip Moreland's name was everywhere in the next few days. It was in the broadsheets and on the lips of Anna Cherton when she came for a visit. Even Willa's seamstress, Miss Brigitte, was spouting out the wonderfulness of his arrival in the Season because his presence had resulted in a number of young women coming by to order new gowns.

Indeed, it was as if London Society had become a seething bed of tittle-tattle. Gossip about his beautiful deceased wife was most prevalent, but so were the stories about the wealth of his estate. People commented endlessly about his handsome looks and easy bearing and about his being so very highborn.

The arrogance he was once accused of was dismissed in favour of his miraculous return and he was not a man it seemed to be censured by anyone. Society now loved him, each rejoinder she heard more flattering than the one before it, and the fact that he was now a widow only added to his allure.

He was the prize catch of the Season and every ambitious mama was out a-hunting.

Wilhelmina went riding five days after seeing the Earl. She needed the exercise and the freedom and she enjoyed the calibre of the horses for rent from the stables in Mount Street. Back at Belton Park horse riding had been the one true escape from all she had to deal with and here in London it had continued to be both a balm and a solace.

Her meeting with Phillip Moreland at the Wilsons' ball had set her on edge. She reasoned it was because she did not know what she expected of him and because their kiss had blurred the lines to such an extent that she was now trying to find ways to actively avoid him.

Thus when coming down the path in Hyde Park and seeing a lone rider in the distance she was shocked to see as she drew closer that it was the much admired Earl of Elmsworth. He wore his hair longer than most did here, the darkness cast into lighter shades today by the first rays of sun as it was ruffled by the wind. There was no way she could ignore him or he her without its appearing most odd and so she pulled her mount to a stop when he was a few feet away.

'My lord.'

'Mrs St Claire. You left the ball the other night before I had the chance to say goodbye.'

'As you were in great demand I hardly thought you would have noticed my absence.'

'I had hoped to ask you for another dance.'

'Most unwise, I fear, sir. Two dances with the same partner on one night might have been remarked upon.'

His returning smile was full of humour and out here in the open air Willa felt her heartbeat race. It was more than disconcerting.

'I was introduced to a close acquaintance of yours after you had left. A Mr George Fitzgibbon.'

She could not quite work out what he was saying, for there was hesitation in his words.

'He thinks very highly of you.'

'He is a good friend.'

'He told me that he had asked for your hand in marriage.'

Shock hit her forcibly. 'And did he relate to you my feelings on the matter?'

'He intimated he was finding it hard to persuade you to answer in the affirmative.'

Willa could not believe that George would be so careless with his confidences.

'Mr Fitzgibbon was foolish in allowing such a

private matter to stray into a public sphere. I should never have made any such confession.'

'Because you value your privacy?'

'I do and I have heard it said that you feel much the same, my lord.'

'Once upon a time I used to worry more about what was said of me but now…' He stopped before going on. 'Now I barely listen to any disapproval.'

'Oh, you need not be concerned. In my experience money and a title talk the loudest of all things. No one would dare criticise you.'

'Even behind my back?'

'Even there, I think. People here do not irritate anyone perceived to have more power than they do.'

'And do you follow such rules, Mrs St Claire?'

'I do, my lord. On the social ladder I have entered upon the very bottom rung. A widow. Untitled. Opinionated. Old. Though moderately wealthy at least, which is one mark in my favour.'

He laughed again and the sound rang out around them, caught on the wind in a singular note.

'How old exactly are you?'

'I am almost thirty-one years old. The age for a woman of no return and well past my prime.'

He did not let her finish.

'You are also, by all accounts, a woman who has turned down many a proposal of marriage?'

'Being a wife never suited me but I have told you that before.'

'At Elmsworth?' His voice was soft.

She looked around. There was no one in front of them or behind. Perhaps it was the hour of the day or the strength of the wind because the park was generally busier. She decided to take a chance.

'I often think of that night, my lord.' She wanted him to know that to her this memory was precious and that she was not ashamed.

He was silent but once she had started she could not just leave it there.

'I often think of it because I am usually far more circumspect. I'm not a wanton woman, my lord, and I should not wish you to think that I might be.'

'I did not.'

'I also do not have a loose tongue like George Fitzgibbon. I would never say anything about what was, after all, a moment only between us. You have made it abundantly clear to me that you do not wish to marry again and I hope I have impressed the same on you, and so….' She stopped, at a loss as to where she might take this next.

Part of her urged a certain daring but the larger part understood that he would not want that. If they had been other people, younger people, less damaged people it might have been easier to take his hand and allow him to know her truer feelings…but they were not those people. Her teeth worried her bottom lip.

'I appreciate your candidness, Mrs St Claire, and I assure you that I likewise would do nothing to ever harm your reputation.'

'I doubt my reputation here is quite as salubrious as you might think it.' She could not help but smile.

He turned his horse into the wind, a beautiful man framed against the trees behind him.

'You do yourself a disservice. I have come across not one person in London who would disparage your name. They admire you. Money has a voice, as you say, I do not doubt it, but true admiration has little to do with the size of a person's fortune. No, it seems you are kind and clever. And joyous,' he added.

She smiled. 'Oh, I do like those words, my lord. Particularly joyous, given I had so many years when I was not.'

She looked so young out here in the breeze and the sun, her golden eyes dancing and her hair full of every shade of brown imaginable. She looked as if she had escaped from the pages of a fairy tale with a happy ending assured and a lifetime of possibility ahead.

No wonder people here were so drawn to her. They wanted the same things that she was full of, the jaded, worn restrictions of London town heavy burdens in the face of such…lightness.

Phillip understood the look in George Fitzgibbon's eyes at that moment in a way he had not before, for Wilhelmina St Claire offered an uncomplicated honesty that was rare.

And she deserved a man who might give her the same back, which was most definitely not him.

Still, he couldn't find it in himself to cut her off completely.

'Your horse looks worn out, Mrs St Claire. How far have you come?'

'Only from Mount Street, Lord Elmsworth.'

'Phillip,' he replied before going on. 'You give the impression of being a fine rider.'

She looked up at the compliment.

'I used to ride at Belton, though my husband had no love of the sport at all.'

'He was too busy searching for stars?'

Her laughter warmed him again.

'I heard that he had named one after you.'

'He found it in the early years of our marriage. I doubt he would have been so generous if such a discovery had been made in the latter ones.'

'What did he die of?'

'He fell from the second storey balcony at Belton Manor. He held on to life for a few wretched hours and then he succumbed, and now when I look at the night sky I apologise.'

'To him?'

'And to our life together. A poor marriage is seldom one person's fault entirely and I had my part in it.'

When he did not speak she elaborated further.

'Lionel was an unhappy man and I lost patience with him. It is hard to be with someone whom you fail so badly to understand, even with all the trying in the world. Which I did, I tried and tried and tried,' she finished off and breathed out heavily. 'Because to me simply giving up is a failure and life is never a perfect thing, no matter how much one would wish it to be.'

How did he do it? How did Phillip Elmsworth make her admit things she had kept inside and hidden for so very, very long?

Her fingers tightened on the reins and she felt overcome. At the unfairness of everything, at the futility, at the sheer impossible sadness of being lost somehow to the sort of life she had wanted.

Her steed was restless beneath her, whickering under restraint, hooves busy on the hard ground.

She saw the Earl noticing too and his next words were exactly what she needed.

'Ride with me to that line of trees over there.'

He pointed to a belt of green oaks a good half-mile on and, digging her heels into the mare's flanks, Willa was away as fast as a side-saddle would allow her. Even though her steed was not the finest, she enjoyed the ride, the rush of breath making her forget any gloominess, so that there seemed to be only them riding for the oaks, only green trees, blue sky and life.

She reached the trees a moment after he did and saw that he'd barely caught a sweat. Still, her mood had lightened and she was grateful for it.

'Who taught you to ride?' His words were soft.

'Mr Henry Matthers. He was a groom at Belton and he'd been a scout in the Peninsular War, riding around armies and across the terrain.'

'He sounds a very useful sort of fellow.'

'And a great talker. He told me the tales of his endeavours for years and even to this day I can recite many of the generals' names and the battles that they fought.'

'What happened to him?'

'Oh, Lionel dismissed him. He was sick of my admiration for Mr Matthers, I think.'

Reining in his stallion, Phillip Moreland picked his way carefully across to her, the elegant lines of his horse on full display as he dismounted, helping her to do the same. She moved back from him as soon as her feet were on the ground, a rush of warmth making her cheeks glow.

'Your horse is clearly a fine ride, my lord.'

'Indeed, though he is not mine. I have a healthy stable at Elmsworth but I have not brought any of the animals from it down with me to London.'

'Because you do not plan to stay long?'

'I don't. I have always enjoyed the country more than the city but there is some business here that I need to attend to.'

Phillip took a breath and tried to relax but today he felt edgy. It was partly because Wilhelmina St Claire looked so very lovely, but it was also a result of not quite knowing what he wanted from this meeting.

'Which stable do you use for your horses in London, Mrs St Claire?'

'Oh, none, my lord, for I no longer have any of the horses I kept at Belton. I only hire horses here.'

'What happened to them?'

'Lionel's cousin took them. I think he felt he should have received more from the estate but Lionel had never stipulated it and…'

'He felt maligned?'

'He was a man who thought women were less than

worthy of any inheritance. Lionel and he had been close once, so…' She shrugged.

'If an estate is not entailed it means it may be distributed in any way the owner requests. There can be no fighting over the letter of the law.'

'Well, that was the trouble really. Mr Simon St Claire thought there was a will other than the one the lawyer produced, an updated will, and a document that allowed him a greater share of everything.'

'So he was disappointed.'

'And angry. When he came to Belton Park and took the horses and quite a number of the family heirlooms in the house I felt powerless to stop him.'

'Damn.'

'He has never contacted me since, though, which is a relief.'

'Was there other family?'

'No, just him, his wife and three sons. It's not as if he was penniless, but he certainly was not as wealthy as Lionel.'

'So astronomy paid well?'

She shook her head. 'Not nearly as well as the metals found in a few of the river valleys of Belton. It allowed Lionel the freedom to dabble at anything he wanted.'

'And what of you? What did you do?'

'I rode when I could.'

'In the hours you were not cleaning the house.'

'You have listened to me well, Lord Elmsworth. I should be more careful with all that I tell you.'

'I am not your enemy, Wilhelmina.'

'I know.'

The air around them changed, a stillness pervading, an awareness of each other that was absolute.

'My mother believed that home is always a place but I am not sure if that is true. Now I might put more weight on people. I imagine it was like that with you and your wife. I hear the stories of your great love…'

She tailed off into silence.

'Gretel and I were young when we met, so in effect we grew up together, learned to understand the world through the same eyes until…' He left a gap and could not continue.

Worry suffused her eyes and Phillip thought this version of Wilhelmina St Claire was a different one than he had seen before.

What had changed? He would have liked to ask, but of course he could not.

'Where did you learn to ride, my lord?' Her words were quiet.

'My father had both my brother and I taught at Elmsworth. Our mother had been afraid of horses, you see, and he wanted us to be different, braver, I suppose, and willing to take risks.'

'And did you?'

He laughed. 'Many times and often with dire consequences. I broke my arm one summer and Oliver broke his collarbone soon after. There were other scrapes, too, but nothing quite as painful. What of you? How old were you?'

'I was twenty-two. It was the freedom of speed that I loved the most at first and then it was the power of it. To go anywhere and be anyone, the wind on your face and your breath whipped into energy. It saved me really because it made everything else bearable, and in the country I did not have to ride side-saddle.'

'Your honesty always surprises me, Mrs St Claire. Usually people are not quite as forthcoming.'

'My parents believed in a silent stoicism and my husband thought contemplation of the universe required a great many hours, so when I left Belton and my former life there I decided that the currency of communication was something I needed as much as air and water to stay alive and sane.'

'I admire such perception of your own needs. Most in society have no understanding of what they require to thrive.'

'Because they are scared to dream? But it's not a

race, I don't think. All truths form in time if you just know how to listen. When Lionel died I left Winchester as soon as I was able and took the road to London without once looking back, and have found a place here that I like and that is mine.'

So certain. He wished he could be like that, someone who could forge a path and follow it to become different. But it was a false hope and an impossible one. He was chained to Elmsworth, to its history and to his title and to all that had happened because of it. He took a step back.

'I have been invited to a masquerade ball to be held at Lord and Lady Duggan's next week. Are you attending?'

'I am, my lord. It is one of the bright spots in the Season's calendar, and a masked soirée is so full of secrets. One can be anything one wants, so there is a certain mystery present, I suppose.'

'I shall not ask what you shall come as, then, Mrs St Claire.'

'And if you did I would not tell you.'

'But I promise I shall track you down there before midnight when the masks are removed.'

She shook her head.

'The Duggans never insist on that. In fact, they normally discourage any revealing whatsoever and everyone goes home as the character they arrived as.'

'An interesting concept.'

'You sound as though you disagree with it.'

'I should think anyone with half a brain should be able to decipher the identity of most people there.'

'I imagined that, too, but it is much harder than you might think. A feigned stoop, a pair of gloves, a voice altered in timbre… There are so many ways to become someone else entirely.'

Such words piqued his interest. 'How would you imagine I could become…incognito?'

She frowned as she considered the question. 'You are always in black, so a brighter colour might do it to begin with.'

'And then…

'Falter a little as you walk. Shorten your steps. Look as though you do not quite fit in.'

He began to laugh again.

'Powder your hair and put it up in a tight queue. Wear an ill-fitting jacket and boots that look scuffed. Find a mask that covers most of your face, and when you speak, do it in a whisper.'

'A complete overhaul, then. Nothing left of me?'

'That's the goal.'

'Should I drink?'

'Only the non-alcoholic punch and very sparingly.'

'And what of dancing?'

'Plead a headache if anyone asks you.'

'Why?'

'I have seen your notable style and so have others.'

'Terrible?'

'The worst. Avoid anyone you are usually seen with…'

She stopped as she said this and began to giggle, a light amusement that turned into laughter, her eyes welling with tears which she wiped away on her sleeve. After a minute of this she took three deep breaths and faced him squarely.

'On second thoughts I believe nothing you could do to hide would be of any use. People will know you because they will be looking for you. It is the great curse of your position here and of your prolonged absence from an estate and a title that is steeped in gossip.'

'Well, I think you are wrong, Mrs St Claire. I believe I should be good at hiding in plain sight.'

'You do?'

'I have just spent years in the Americas being more people than can be counted on two hands and never once being caught out.'

'Were you a spy there?'

'Of course not.'

'An actor in a circus, then?'

'No.'

'A cowboy. A preacher. A gunslinger.'

Phillip could not remember a conversation he had

enjoyed more as he shook his head to each one of her outlandish suggestions, and without meaning to he told her the truth.

'I was simply running away from myself.'

That stopped her mirth as nothing else could and she was quiet. Waiting.

'A very hard thing to do?'

'The hardest.'

'I know that because I did the same.'

He reached out for her hand and brought it into his.

'Yet now you live well?'

'I do.'

He looked away but did not drop her fingers. Rather, he cradled them closer.

'Thank you for today.' The words were torn from the innermost part of him.

There were more people on the paths now in the distance and he could see his manservant on a horse cantering towards them.

He had asked him to do this to allow him an escape in case…

He cursed under his breath and let her go, the wind rising between them and the sky returning to grey.

Jamming his hands in his pockets, he watched as Bates came closer.

Every time she saw the Earl of Elmsworth Willa was more bewildered. It was if he had a certain amount of hours to give her before some invisible clock struck twelve and like Cinderella he fled away.

From her. From the truth. From a conversation that might expose him.

But his laughter had not been forced and the jesting between them had been…she tried to think of the right word. Real? Genuine? Exhilarating? A connection that had felt just the same as in the kitchens of Elmsworth.

He'd held her hand to warm it against his coat and she'd known the heavy beat of his heart. Steady. Constant. That of a man who had stood against the forces that had been thrown against him and survived.

Chapter Five

Phillip came awake with a familiar dread, the years-ago horror of the gunshot reverberating in all corners of his mind. His finger on the trigger and Oliver falling, Gretel by his side, her face flushed, her eyes aglow, and the words she had uttered ones that could never be taken back.

Sitting up and leaning over, he tried to find the breath that he had lost, tried to piece himself together, tried to stop the trembling.

Shaking his head hard, he got out of bed, opening the curtains to let in some light. A half-moon at least. He bathed in the glow with relief, feeling his heartbeat slow, feeling that scene in the Elmsworth library fade.

The cry of a small child in a room along the corridor was welcomed. There was other life here, fragile but real. He longed for a further wail but there was only silence.

His brother, his wife and their two sons had arrived at the town house in the late afternoon, their eldest son having broken his arm and Esther wanting it to be seen by the Elmsworth physician in town. Phillip liked that he could hear even in the middle of the night some sound of life, which promised comfort. He wondered where the little girl was, the one with the doll. He searched his memory for a name. Juliette.

'Wherefore art thou, Juliette?' he whispered to himself, his small attempt at humour another ease.

He would not sleep again now. Two o'clock. A long way until dawn and no chance of wandering the house, as was his usual habit, with his brother's family close.

Placing his open palm on the coldness of the glass, he watched the shadow of condensation grow around it in an outline of himself as he tried to recall the scent of Wilhelmina St Claire. Flowers. Gardenias and violets. He had always been good at recognising scents. Other things were there too. Cinnamon and a touch of mint. Did she concoct her own perfume? Gretel had favoured bergamot and musk, heavier aromas, the suggestion of odours much more defined than the ones Mrs St Claire preferred.

Occasionally even now, he would walk through the London town house and imagine faint tinges of his wife's scent in the quieter corners of the place. Sometimes he gulped in the recall of her and other times he held his breath until he was sure she had gone.

He remembered back to the first time he had met Gretel and how at the end of the evening at the Westinghouse ball she had placed her dainty hand on his sleeve as they walked alone on a greenery-filled balcony and poured her heart out to him.

'You make me feel so very at home in your company, my lord, a safe harbour if you will, a place to rest.'

These unforgettable words had been like a marvellous gift to him, for he'd never truly had a home before and certainly not one that was safe. With her beauty, softness and her smile he'd felt his future sealed; it had been such an easy choice and such a quick certainty.

It was only later that he'd understood that Gretel was like a fragile hothouse flower who needed more care and tenderness to survive than any man would ever be able to give her.

The wail from the baby sounded for a second time, muffled by someone rising to comfort him. Esther, he thought, her night punctured by the infant's restlessness. He wondered if his own mother had ever got up for him or had he been fobbed off to the help?

If he had a son, he would want the child to experience so much more love than he'd been raised on. He swore then, softly. He would not marry again. He would produce no heir for Elmsworth. He would die without issue and the estate would revert to Oliver and his progeny.

Shaking his head again, Phillip thought back to his encounter with Wilhelmina St Claire. He had never enjoyed a ride as much before with such wide breadths of conversation. He frowned because such a thought was a betrayal to his wife, but there it was, admitted. He liked the way Wilhelmina laughed and the way she teased him.

She had told him in no uncertain terms that she would never marry again and that she was not looking for a husband. But there was something between them that was different; something that made his heart beat faster and gave parts of his body a life he had not felt possible for years.

Lord. His fingers threaded through his hair and he swore roundly. She was making him into a man he did not recognise, a man who wanted things that could not come true.

Esther's first cousin, Miss Arabella Montague, arrived at the town house in the early afternoon in the company of her brother, Theodore Montague, and his new wife, Stella, and on seeing her Phillip understood why his sister-in-law had arranged this meeting. One glance at Oliver's face confirmed his suspicions. They wanted him to find a wife. They wanted him to have what they had. *A nest.* Wilhelmina's words rolled around in his head as he was introduced.

'I am so very pleased to meet you, Lord Elmsworth, for the tales of your travels in America have fuelled in me a desire to follow in your footsteps.'

'A bold proposal.'

He wondered how she would get there and who she would go with.

'I can see in your expression that you think that I will not manage this, my lord.' Her eyes were the colour of cornflowers and her lips turned up. A woman who was used to the adulation of men, he surmised, and expected it.

'I am not quite as timid as other girls here in England are required to be. My beleaguered father would attest to that.' Her laugh was practised and he smiled back because she probably was waiting for such a reaction and because humour defused the exasperation he was beginning to feel. With care he glanced at his watch. Three-thirty. How long before he could plead another engagement and leave?

'America is a big place, Miss Montague, and one

where as a foreigner it might be easy to misunderstand the lay of the land.' If she was being honest about her will to travel she would need to be warned of difficulties.

'Oh, I am sure she would not be travelling alone, Phillip.' This interjection came from Esther. 'Her father for one would never countenance such a journey.'

Arabella shook her head with a rueful exasperation at her cousin's words. 'And it is such a shame that this should be the case, given men can travel in any way they please and as far as their heart's content whilst women can venture nowhere at all alone. What of you, my lord, will you ever return to America?'

'I doubt it. The estate keeps me busy here and years on the road have dulled my quest for more travel.'

'I think I should be the exact opposite. I think once I start on such a journey I should never wish to leave it.'

'A perpetual traveller?'

'Well, you may question my motives but I assure you what I say is the truth.'

Phillip could see that Arabella Montague was disappointed with him, disappointed with his answers and his lack of interest. Esther was also looking at him with puzzlement.

This is me now, he felt like saying. *I am numb to all beauty in the world.* Unexpectedly he thought of Gretel and wished she were here. At least his wife knew his demons.

Oliver's observation changed things again. 'The world is a big place, Arabella, and I am sure there are many wonderful sights for you to safely enjoy.'

Miss Montague was quick to reply.

'Exactly, and I have a great ambition to go to see as much as I can before I am very much older.'

Phillip raised his glass, even as he wondered how old she was. She looked impossibly young. 'Then I wish you well on your quest. My thirst for such things is past but yours is just beginning.' He could hear the hollowness of such words.

'Mrs Wilhelmina St Claire said much the same thing to me at the Wilsons' ball the other night,' Theodore Montague countered. 'Not about travel so much but about life.'

Esther looked puzzled. 'That does not sound like Mrs St Claire at all. She is usually far more…daring.'

'Perhaps a woman who invites discourse and debate into her salons needs to relax into caution sometimes?' Arabella Montague's brother uttered this almost as a question, though Oliver interrupted him.

'Since arriving in London Mrs St Claire has become a force in her own right, so I imagine she has little time for such excessive introspection.'

'And yet Society prefers women to be…less forceful, does it not?' There was censure in the words.

'This is exactly what I am talking about, Theo. It is just so unfair and unreasonable.' Arabella Montague sounded cross.

'Rules are there as a protection, dear sister, especially for the fairer sex, as there are so many ways you can be hurt.'

Esther now took up the cause. 'I am afraid, Theodore, that I have to agree with Arabella, which is why the actions of women such as Mrs St Claire are so valuable.' Although his sister-in-law smiled, her words held an undercurrent of steel. 'It's a changing world and women are leading the charge.'

'"…we know what we are, but know not what we may be."' Phillip's voice was soft.

'You read Shakespeare?' Esther asked this with wonder.

'Gretel did and often. I think she read me every play the Bard ever wrote and great parts of it I can recite at obscure times like this,' he returned.

'Which is quite a gift, I should imagine.'

Her unusual eyes twinkled as if she was laughing at him. But he could not take umbrage, for there was an energy about Esther that was catching. Arabella and her party, on the other hand, were watching them all as if they could barely understand a word said.

Like a play, each character caught by their own realities and experiences. He wished the wonder in his sister-in-law and the naive innocence of Arabella Montague were still there inside of him, but they were long gone.

Oliver probably felt the same. Glancing over, he saw his brother frowning. There had been a time when they knew what the other was thinking, when they'd cowered together under bedcovers in the night for fear that their mother might come to rail them with her constant anger. Aye, there had been a time when it was them against the world; the Moreland boys pitted against parents who were not coping with secrets that could never be allowed to escape.

Phillip remembered thinking as a boy that perhaps every family was damaged in ways that were opaque to outsiders, and that the pain lingering in his own was a normal occurrence. He had thought that until the boat trip on the lake, one grey afternoon at Elmsworth.

Then he'd known there were problems that neither he, nor his brother, nor his father could ever fix. Space was the only thing that had calmed his anxiety, the space to be away from the others, the space he gained at boarding school, tucked into the dormitory with forty other boys and safe from things at home.

When Oliver had joined him at Eton, Phillip had shunned him largely, not wanting the fear relived or the secrets rehashed. Oliver presumably had felt the same, and Gretel had cemented the distance between them, for, as an only child, she had felt no compunction to form alliances with what was left of his broken family.

And now…?

The bonds of adversity were after all not such easy things to cast away. Here Phillip knew that, despite their differences, the person who understood him the best was Oliver. He took in a deep breath as Miss Montague spoke again.

'Mrs St Claire should take care with her opinions, though, for even a wealthy older widow can garner resentment for being so different.'

Her brother nodded, and for a second Phillip saw what he had not before: Wilhelmina St Claire was as much of an outsider here in Society as he felt, only she did not care. She hurried into her life to catch up on all that she had missed in a way that was completely original, and used joy as a shield. Lionel St

Claire may have stolen ten years of her life but she was damned if anyone would steal the rest.

He remembered her words in the park, her humour and her irreverence. She was bound by no one and tempered only with freedom. That was her beauty and it was so much more forceful than the pallid prettiness of Arabella Montague.

When a servant appeared with a tray of tea and cakes Phillip was grateful. The fare had brought other, lighter topics to the fore. The inclement weather. The upcoming masquerade ball. The projected plans outlining the improvements to the grand entrance at Hyde Park Corner. Relaxing, he sat back to listen to the general conversation and debate, glad he was not pulled in to contribute to it.

After his brother and family departed the next morning Phillip spent the afternoon looking into the affairs of the Moreland investments. The portfolio he perused was a hefty and healthy one, for his father, although having many failings at the personal level, had always been an astute businessman.

It was almost five o'clock and the first shadows of the evening were beginning to strip the light from the room when a familiar voice echoed in the corridor outside his room and he stood.

His aunt Julia, complete with a large-brimmed

hat, gloves and coat, was almost running towards him, a wide smile on her face.

'Phillip. My goodness. I had heard that you were back in England but I could hardly believe it.'

She wrapped her arms around him, holding on tightly, the two servants in the passageway looking around in interest.

'I might say the same of you. Oliver was sure you were in France until the end of summer, Julia.'

His aunt smiled. 'I was supposed to be but I found myself getting a little lonely on the edge of the south coast despite all of the social occasions. I wanted to be home and so I found a passage, arriving yesterday. But look at you!' She stood back a little. 'You look healthy, my love, and happy, and I have heard you have even graced a few Society events in the past weeks.'

'I can always count on you to be well informed of the latest gossip, Julia, even if you have only been back in England for a matter of hours.'

'It pays to keep one's eyes open in the melee that is Society, would you not say? But enough of all this. I want to tell you how sorry I was for the loss of your wife. I hope it was easy at the end for you both.'

'Death is seldom easy in any form and I do recall that you and Gretel never truly got on.'

'We were not enemies, Phillip, but then again, unfortunately, we were not friends either. It is just that your wife was a woman who found it hard to share you with anyone.'

'You are saying she was too insular?'

'No, I don't think I am quite saying that. I think I mean that she would have been happier had she allowed others to know her. Your mother held that same habit of drawing in. As her sister I always felt Miranda was distant and people who shy away from social gatherings are often lonely even without recognising it.'

'You sound like Oliver. He told me the same thing when I went to see him at Nettleford Park.'

'That is because he is bathing in the glowing happiness of a perfect match.'

Phillip expected this sentiment from his aunt but today he just did not want to hear it, though as he turned away Julia stopped him.

'I do not mean to undermine Gretel, Phillip, for I know how much you loved her and I wish she had not been sick. Oh, how I wish it. But here is your chance, now, to find a partner who might allow you a new life. God knows every young girl in Society and their mothers must have you in their sights.'

'I don't want another marriage.'

'Yet Elmsworth needs heirs.'

'Which Oliver has provided.'

Her smile was sad. 'Your father would be turning in his grave if he could hear that.'

'He loved you, Julia.' It was a relief to change the subject even as his aunt turned a bright red. 'Once he told me he wished he had asked you to marry him instead of Miranda.'

'Your mother was not an easy woman, but she was fearful, and no matter what she did to try and get herself better she just could not.'

'She tried to kill us. Twice.' He heard the tremble in his words.

'Oliver told me the same thing and it is a large burden for any son to carry, but she was sick, Phillip, sicker than any of us realised.'

'I tried to save her before she drowned in the lake, but the water was too cold.'

'And you were ill for months after. We thought you would be lost too.'

'I don't remember that.'

'You were the one who always tried to glue your family together, Phillip, despite great odds. Oliver gave up years before you did. He simply let everyone go.'

'I'd forgotten how forthright you always are, Aunt Julia.'

'I just want to see you happy. You deserve to be at least that after all you have been through.'

'Happiness holds many shades.'

'I understand that better than you know. When your father told me that he would never leave Miranda I thought I might die of sorrow. But as you can well see I did not and life crept in despite my wishing that it wouldn't and my world came back into a shape that was manageable.'

This was a different answer than he might have expected and a useful one. 'What was it that helped you do this?'

'People. I got out and I let people in. I decided that I was too young to simply give up and that in every conversation I would find something to help me. Surprisingly I did. I took a risk and a chance and it paid off and after some months I could barely recognise the woman I had been.' She stopped and smiled at him. 'Actually I have been asked to the fiftieth birthday of Esther's aunt next week and it is a masquerade ball. It is sometimes easier to be a new version of yourself when one is disguised, and besides, you can so easily slip away if you do not find it enjoyable.'

The vein of his aunt's words was so similar to that which Wilhelmina had pursued he had to smile.

'I hope you will stay for a drink and a light supper and tell me all about your travels on the Continent.'

Chapter Six

Phillip had come as Hades, Lord of the Underworld, his mask a full one in black ceramic and his hair hidden beneath a wild and tangled wig.

He could barely identify himself and was certain he would not be recognised without much difficulty.

He'd chosen the Unseen One because he liked the hiddenness of such a god and because his father had had the ceramic mask made for himself years ago. He'd borrowed his father's clothes, too. They were large and shapeless and hid even more of him, just as Willa had predicted.

He wondered what she would come as, for he had not seen her after the ride in the park anywhere, even though he had made himself attend both the Countess of Luxton's ball and the Smithsons' Mayfair party the following week in the hope of running into her.

He'd toyed with the idea of sending her a note to

ask if everything was all right but decided against it. He wished Oliver and Esther might have still been in London so that he could have slipped Willa's name into a conversation and gleaned some information about her movements. But his brother and wife had stayed with him only briefly before hurrying back to Nettleford Park.

So he was here on his own, a solitary dark-garbed figure in a mask with a confusing excitement that welled inside him. He wanted to see Wilhelmina St Claire and talk with her as he had the other week in the park. He wanted her laughter and her irreverence and that particular smile of hers which said *I know more about you than you want to tell me but I will be kind.*

Shaking his head, he wondered if perhaps he was sick or tired. But it wasn't either of those because he felt more alive than he had felt in a long while, and the feeling came down to his time in her company.

There were hundreds of people here, he realised as he stepped inside, the ball spreading over three or four large salons that stretched into the distance, the mirrors around the walls widening the space yet again.

His heart sank. There was no way he would be able to find anyone in this melee and so he took an offered drink from the serving minotaur as a distraction.

The Duggans knew their wine, was his next thought, and the night looked up.

His aunt Julia crossed before him a few yards away dressed in an outlandish sea-goddess costume. He was pleased when she did not recognise him. Further afield he could see Miss Arabella Montague surrounded by every manner of masculine fairy folk and Greek deity. She had made little attempt to hide her beautiful face and was easily identifiable.

An hour later a figure in a flowing mantle passed him by, carrying a wreath of leaves. The banded tiara of gold and green on her head was joined to a white mask but it was the notes of gardenia and violets that caught his attention. He watched her for a moment quietly stalking around the edges of the room and refusing the offered glass of wine as she did so. No one joined her, which was an oddness in itself as at every social occasion Wilhelmina was more normally within a tight group of friends.

He saw her scan the room back and forth until her glance came over him, caught across the width of the salon, noise and lights flickering and the sounds of a small orchestra tuning their instruments.

She had seen him somehow, under the ceramic mask and the clothes and the wig. His height probably had something to do with it but there were other things also at play. He watched her as she threaded through the throng to stand beside him, lifting her mask slightly to identify herself.

'The Hidden God is an entirely appropriate costume, my lord.'

'What gave me away?'

'Your stillness. Everyone in the room is moving and you are stationary. I have seen that before in you.'

His glance ran over the green-and-white silk mantle she wore. 'You are Daphne?'

'The tree spirit?' She shook her head. 'Try again.'

'Demeter? Persephone?'

'Wrong on all counts, although you do get full marks for your knowledge of the goddesses of natural things. I am Nike, the Goddess of Victory.'

'Minus the wings.'

'Pardon?'

'I thought Nike sported wings. You have none.'

At that she laughed. 'You do surprise me, Lord Elmsworth, with the scope of your general knowledge.'

Julia had joined them now, finally recognising him, her hand resting on his arm in familiarity.

'My goodness, Phillip. Is that you? I would never

have guessed in a million years had it not been for your father's mask.'

'Do you know Mrs St Claire?' he then asked.

Turning to Willa, Julia lifted her mask of seaweed so that a part of her face was visible.

'I do, having attended a few of her wonderful evenings of discussion in the past few years. It is so nice to see you again, Wilhelmina, for I often thought of you in Nice as I perused the art galleries of that city.'

'A veritable treat, Lady Julia.'

'You have been there, too, then? To France?'

Willa shook her head. 'No, I have not, but I have heard wonderful stories.'

The orchestra then burst into life. Another waltz and, wanting some time alone with Wilhelmina, Phillip asked her to dance. As they stepped away he saw a wide smile on Julia's face.

'Your aunt looks content.'

'She has learnt the difficult trick of living a happy life and wants others to do the same.' His hand came around her back, pressing her in, here amongst the gods and the warriors and fairy folk.

'Is it not such a relief to suspend the conventions of polite Society, my lord?'

Her question ran alongside his own thoughts.

'Fifty years ago these affairs were even more risque. Imagine that.' Her voice held humour.

A man in a long cloak of black pushed past, a thin mask serving as the sole means of disguise. Beside him strode a jester, fully costumed from head to foot, the Harlequin pattern of his clothing reflected in the material of a hood pulled tight across his face.

'All kinds of people like to hide,' she said this quietly, 'and it is not often that they have the chance to do so.'

He could see Julia watching him, and further afield Arabella Montague watched them too. Society had its eyes wide open even in incognito and he knew he needed to be careful. Shifting back, he took a breath.

'I have not seen you at any of the Society events across the last week.'

'That's because I have barely been out.'

'Have you been ill?'

'No, merely preoccupied with the affairs of my estate.'

'That sounds ominous.'

She smiled. 'Lawyers always are, my lord.'

'Is everything all right?'

She stopped and looked at him directly.

'It is.'

Phillip Moreland's hand was warm against her own. She noticed that those around them were starting to recognise his true identity. Her disguise was nowhere near as complete as his and yet in his company the more astute patrons were beginning to put them together.

When Arabella Montague crossed over towards them as the waltz came to an end she knew that their quiet isolation was over. The group of men and women accompanying Miss Montague looked quizzical until she spoke his name.

'Lord Elmsworth. I wondered if you would come tonight. Mrs St Claire.'

This was said with far less enthusiasm.

Willa had never been able to understand women who saw every other female as a threat and especially not those as beautiful as Arabella Montague. The young woman had donned a flimsy half-mask which barely covered any of the features of her face.

'I had promised my aunt Julia that I would at least make an appearance.'

'You are in London for a while longer, then?'

'Perhaps.'

He did not expand on his answer, leaving a small but awkward gap in the conversation.

'I heard that you are about to travel to France, Miss Montague?' Willa asked the question to fill the silence.

'Indeed, I am. Mr Fitzgibbon is to accompany our

party. It seems he has a great affection for the region and is in dire need of cheering up.'

The last words were said in an accusing tone but Willa ignored them altogether. She could not be responsible for George's melancholy, and the three letters he had sent her in the last week had been full of the emotion.

Lionel had needed constant propping up, too, and she had sworn never to do that again in any relationship.

'Well, I hope the weather is warm and the skies are sunny in the south, Miss Montague. At this time of the year I hear they generally are.'

An innocuous reply but she had found talk of the weather always invoked a kind of natural end to conversations and indeed it was only a moment or two before Arabella and her group swanned off again.

'Well done, Mrs St Claire.'

His words were filled with humour.

'I rather think she hoped she might have had you to herself, my lord.'

'It has been centuries since I felt that young and untroubled.'

'Difficulties in life mark one, I expect, which is why these masked balls hold so much attraction.'

He laughed out loud and she liked the sound. She might never know his trials, and he might never learn of hers, but for now as the music began again she walked into his arms for the next dance.

It was improper, she knew. One ought not to allow more than a few dances to one partner and certainly not two in a row, but if people were noticing she chose not to look. Phillip Moreland felt warm and safe and large, a man who could beat the memory of everything away at least for an evening.

He had lifted his mask upwards now so that the arch of it sat at his forehead, allowing her to see his eyes. He watched the crowd around them, never fully at ease, and she wondered what had made him so guarded.

There were so many parts to one's life that could scar a person.

He still wore his wedding ring. There was a long white mark on his neck beneath his ear on the left side. He favoured his left leg in the dance as well, for she could feel the slight shift of weight as he moved into particular steps. And the tremor she felt in his hand was there each time they touched.

That was the only thing he did not hide. Perhaps it was so much a part of him he had forgotten about it, an affliction normalised by the length of its existence.

'You are quiet.' His eyebrows were raised.

'I was trying to decide who you are, my lord, underneath the disguise.'

'Do people have to be something different, Mrs St Claire?'

'To my knowledge they almost always are. Take Miss Annabelle, for instance. She is beautiful and clever but she is also frightened. Of time perhaps and its passing.'

'And what of you? What is it that you conceal?'

'Oh, a thousand things like everybody else probably. My disappointments are no surprise as I have already told you some of those.'

'Your husband?'

Willa hated the anger that she felt at his question. He could not know just what she had lost. No one ever would.

But a public ball was no place for such private anguish and so with intent she looked about her, finding something else entirely different to say.

'I had imagined your brother and his wife would have been here tonight celebrating with Esther's aunt and uncle.'

'Their eldest son broke his arm and has been sick with an infection, so they have remained at Nettleford Park. He is regaining his health, though, from the latest reports.'

'Do you visit them there? It is not such a far distance.'

'I have but…' He stopped and frowned and then began again. 'You spoke of different paths in life. Well, Oliver has found his own way and he is happy.'

She knew exactly what he meant.

'And now you have to have the space to find yours?'

'People believe you have an uncanny knack of saying just the right thing, Mrs St Claire. It seems you cultivate much respect in a city not known for its empathy towards others.'

'Oh, that's one of the nicest things anyone has ever said to me, Lord Elmsworth.'

'Then you take it as a truth?'

'No, I take it as a compliment.'

They were quiet then, feeling the rhythm of their movements, and Willa decided that she had been a little harsh in her criticism of his style of dancing. Tonight the steps were easier, their bodies moving as one. She wished they might stay this way forever, in costumes that allowed them some covering from others and from themselves.

He smelt of soap and there was some other scent there that was hard to discern. Camphor perhaps, from the old clothes he wore. She liked that he was not the same as other men she knew who lathered themselves in heavy perfumes and potent girlish creams.

It was strange, for she had known the Earl for such a short time and yet she felt she knew him better than Lionel, whom she'd had to endure for years. There was sadness, too. If only she had found a man like Phillip Moreland when she was young. A man she liked to listen to and whom she enjoyed talking with. An interesting man who obviously read widely and was worldly wise. Her hand tightened on his and he looked down.

'Sorry.' She loosened her grip and he smiled.

'Usually I hate dancing, but with you it is easier. Did you come to London much during your marriage?'

'Oh, hardly ever. Though I've told you already that I saw you once a long time ago at the Merryweather ball. I saw your wife briefly, too, and she was very beautiful.'

'Gretel and I married young and sometimes I think that was a…' He stopped himself but she knew what he was going to say.

A mistake.

Breathing in, she wondered if he might go on but he did not and the gold in his wedding ring on his left hand glinted under the light of the chandeliers.

Shutting her eyes, she banished all introspection.

Just enjoy now, she thought, now in his arms, their fingers entwined, the feel of him against her, strong and tall.

She could not remember a time when she had ever felt so safe.

When the music ended they threaded their way through the crowd.

The Earl of Hammond joined them as they stood to one side of the room, his sister still in tow. Benjamin Harcourt was near by dressed as a Roman god and on seeing Phillip came straight over, his face swathed in a smile.

'It is so good to have you back in England, Phillip.' He looked next at Wilhelmina and tipped his head. 'Mrs St Claire, it is lovely to see you, too. Phillip and I were friends at Eton and in the holidays he often came back to my family estate in Richmond to stay.'

'And some of those holidays were the best times of my life, Ben. How are your parents?'

Ben's smile faded. 'Both dead, I am afraid. Papa of a heart attack and mama from sadness a few months later.'

'I am sorry.'

'No, don't be. It is better that way as they are together.' He pointed to the ceiling. 'Up there, I imagine, and still laughing.'

'And your sister?'

'Married a laird from outside Glasgow and now has four rambunctious red-haired children whom we see often.'

'A good life, then.' Phillip had always enjoyed the dynamics of the Harcourt family with humour evident and love paramount. So unlike his own life.

'You must visit us in Richmond. I am married now and we have two small children.'

Life had moved on for everyone, not just for Oliver.

'Perhaps you could come as well, Mrs St Claire. Sarah, my wife, has often spoken of you, though she was unable to be here tonight.'

'Sarah Harcourt?' Wilhelmina sounded intrigued. 'Oh, I would like that, for your wife has visited my house a few times to join in the discussions and she was always interesting.'

'She does have a mind of her own but I've encouraged that.'

Phillip saw Wilhelmina beaming at Benjamin, a man who wore his heart on his sleeve without any hesitation.

Why had he lost touch? he thought next, and knew the answer as soon as he had finished thinking it. Because Gretel had liked neither Benjamin nor his wife, finding them too outspoken and Bohemian.

She preferred people like her, quiet and refined, which had narrowed down their social outings dramatically. Towards the end there'd hardly been any at all.

'If you would like to it would be our pleasure to host you both at Summerley. The gardens are very beautiful at this time of the year.'

When Wilhelmina nodded, Benjamin looked more than happy, and Phillip was grateful for the invitation.

Others joined them now and they formed a large group on the side of the ballroom, many of the disguises lifted away to reveal the identity of the person beneath. Lord and Lady Duggan were a part of it, an interesting couple who were gracious and welcoming. Phillip couldn't remember being in Society ever being this simple before, and as Wilhelmina stayed in place beside him he decided a large part of the ease was because of her.

After two o'clock he escorted her to her carriage on the circular driveway before the imposing Duggan town house. He had removed his mask completely now and she had too in readiness to say goodbye.

But an awkwardness settled between them which had not been there at all in the evening. He wondered what she might think if he took the back of her hand

and kissed it but she had both hands deeply embedded in the large pockets of her cloak, so he did not step forward.

Seeing the footman waiting a few yards away to help her in, he bowed his head and moved back.

'Goodnight.' She smiled and moved away as he watched her alight the small steps and disappear into the carriage.

Her face through the glass was momentarily caught in the light and then she was gone. Phillip did not return to the ball but made his way to his own carriage further down the street.

He'd been in London for nearly two whole weeks and was not desperate to be back in Hampshire. That thought amazed him.

Chapter Seven

Mr Thomas Sampson from Gates and Wilcox, the legal firm that Lionel had always used, came to see Wilhelmina the afternoon after the Duggans' masquerade ball.

He was a tall and serious man and she felt that from the first moment of meeting him she was on the back foot.

'The estate you wish to sell, Mrs St Claire, is unfortunately tied up in a caveat from your late husband's cousin. Mr Simon St Claire has asked for a stay while he goes through his brother's papers just to make certain that Belton Park is indeed legally yours to sell.'

'The house was not entailed and I was Lionel's wife for eleven years. The will I saw after his death was unencumbered.'

'Mr Simon St Claire isn't…how shall I say it…an easy man? We have had dealings with him over the past year and a half and he is a difficult client who likes to get his own way.'

'And if he doesn't?'

'I for one should not wish to cross him personally and you are alone here and a woman…' He left it at that.

'Tell him to present his evidence, Mr Sampson, within a month. Otherwise I shall sell the house to anybody I want to.'

'I will make sure to relate that to him, Mrs St Claire. Oh, and I almost forgot, one of my colleagues, Mr Elliott MacDonald, also asked me to send you his regards.'

Willa bit down on an answer. Did Mr Sampson know anything of their history? Was this another roundabout threat? But it seemed the man had completed all he had come to say as he stood and bade her farewell.

'I will return in a month and let you know the outcome of all of this. I sincerely hope that this matter shall be resolved in your favour and if there is any movement on the matter I shall also send word.'

'Thank you.'

Willa waited as he left and then sat on the chair by the window, watching the leaves of the trees in the garden shifting in the wind. She had delayed on the sale of Belton Park for just this very reason. She knew Lionel's family was not happy at all with her inheritance of the house, for she had had various legal correspondence outlining all their grievances. But this was the first time they had sent one of their lawyers to visit her and, from what Mr Sampson said, their anger constituted a threat.

It was as if Lionel himself had come back again to make her life difficult, a further harassment just as things were beginning to fall into place. Mr Elliott MacDonald, a lawyer, had been one of her worst mistakes in those dreadful days after Lionel's death. Desperate for some comfort, she had turned to him and the close contact was like an elixir. He was kind, thoughtful and clever and a kiss they had shared had led to much more with all of her heightened emotions after Lionel's death. When he departed a day later she'd never heard from him again, the shame and stupidity of their brief encounter all that she now remembered.

She had been so happy this morning, waking to a blue day with the promise of a visit down to Richmond to see the lovely gardens of the Harcourts. And now…

She could not tell the Earl anything of this history, for there were so many parts of her past that she did not want Phillip Moreland to know.

Perhaps she should simply sign the house over

to Simon St Claire to be forever rid of him and his threats? Perhaps she should leave London altogether and start again somewhere else? Somewhere different? Somewhere far, far away? She had money in a London bank account under her own name that would last for many years if she was careful, and yet she could not simply disappear.

She had spent ten years as the wife of Lionel St Claire and a good many of them had been miserable. To just give up and run without some sort of fight was a coward's way of doing it, and the feeling of excitement she had in Phillip Moreland's company was so life affirming. But with the delay of a month on the sale of Belton there was also no time to waste.

Standing, she walked to the table to pick up the bell and rang it, her butler appearing almost immediately.

'Could you call a carriage around in an hour, please, as I need to go out?'

Phillip was reading in his study when his man came in with a visitor card.

'Mrs Wilhelmina St Claire, sir.'

He stood at this unexpected news and pulled a jacket on, tidying his hair with his hand after he had done so.

'Show her in, please.'

This afternoon Wilhelmina was dressed in a riding jacket and split skirt, her hair pulled up under a hat and tied at the back of her neck in a loose net.

'My lord.' Her greeting was formal. 'I should have sent a letter but I decided this was easier. Last night at the ball Mr Harcourt extended an invitation to view the gardens at his estate in Richmond. He intimated the flowers were at their best and most fragrant and I have decided I would very much like to see such a sight.'

'When were you thinking of making this trip?' He could not quite keep the surprise from his voice.

'I thought this week might be a good time. I know I should not be here asking if I could come along but the invitation was to both of us and you did look as if you accepted the offer.'

'I did, for was there not some urgency in it with the flowers at their peak for only a small amount of time?'

Her smile heartened him. 'Exactly. He said the beds of iris will be wilting in only a matter of a week.'

'So what day and time would you like to travel to Richmond? I could take my carriage out there.'

'You would do that?' She could not believe his words, especially after the horrible start to her day.

But then, Phillip Moreland had that habit of making everything easy, fun and safe.

The Harcourt house, Summerley Court, was exactly as Phillip remembered it, a slightly run-down Tudor mansion outside of Richmond, its gardens of wild flowers interspersed with more formal flowerbeds in front of the long and elegant double-storey building.

Wilhelmina and he had spoken of the weather and the countryside on the way across and of other lesser things, but the conversation had been more stilted than usual, which was probably due to the fact of being alone in a small space together for a few hours.

Certainly the teasing he was more used to in her company was missing and he wished it back.

Benjamin and Sarah Harcourt came to meet them the moment their carriage drew into the driveway, giving the impression that they had been waiting for their guests to come.

Phillip watched as Wilhelmina made sure her hat was on firmly after checking to see the tendrils of her hair were not coming loose. When the door opened and they stepped out, Sarah Harcourt enveloped Wilhelmina.

'Welcome to Summerley. It is such a pleasure to have you both here. When my husband informed me yesterday that you were coming to visit us I could hardly believe it.'

Wilhelmina hugged her back as she laughed at such an effusive greeting. Ben pumped Phillip's hand up and down, his grip strong.

'I think Sarah has looked forward to your arrival more than any guests we have ever had.'

'I used to love coming to your discussions in London, Mrs St Claire. They filled me with ideas and hopes and you were always so very kind.'

'Please call me Willa,' she said, and accepted a bunch of colourful fragrant lilacs and roses handed to her wrapped in a sacking cloth.

'Oh, they are lovely. I hope they will keep so that I might take them home for my front parlour.'

'We will put them in water until you are ready to depart. But now you must come in and meet our children.'

An hour later they were all sitting outside in the familiar long cane loungers, much more tatty than Phillip remembered from his youth but very comfortable. A maid had brought out cool drinks and a plate of assorted small cakes and sandwiches. The talk now was of their childhood adventures and all the various scrapes they seemed to have got into. Ben had a much better recall of the time than he did.

'You always seemed to arrive looking thin and with some injury but by the end of the summer you had filled out and were full of health.'

'Well, that's because your mother fed us more food than I had ever seen in my life and it was always delicious.'

'She used to make us matching outfits, too, because you never brought enough clothes, and we'd roam the land as the matching Merry Men of Robin Hood or the knights of old. There were so many characters I can hardly remember them all.'

'I think I still have many of those old outfits in a trunk at Elmsworth.'

Phillip wondered privately if the senior Mrs Harcourt had ever gleaned the sort of mother his own was and had tried to make it up for him. He imagined she had, on reflection, for he was always sent back with much more than he had ever brought with him and she had made sure he had a standing invitation for the next holiday period.

'How long were you at school together?' Wilhelmina asked this softly.

Benjamin began to speak again. 'From ten until we left Eton at eighteen. After that we lost touch somehow, but you had married Gretel Carmichael and you were busy with your wife and the estate and all that entailed. I did try to come across to Elmsworth Manor to see you but it was difficult to find a time that worked, and then at twenty-two I travelled with my family to the Continent before coming back and meeting Sarah.'

'Can you believe we first saw each other at Lackingtons both reaching for a book of the maps of England?' There was humour in Sarah's words. 'Like the gentleman he was, he allowed me the copy and we sat and talked for hours. How is it that you two met?'

'Mrs St Claire and her party dropped into Elmsworth on their way to London.' Phillip Moreland gave a vague answer but Wilhelmina expanded on it.

'I was most ill from a meal I had consumed on the way and one of my travelling companions insisted we stop in at Elmsworth Manor to get help.'

'We met only briefly that first time but afterwards I saw her in London.' Phillip's description was so very different from the reality that Willa horrifyingly felt the blood run to her face in a burning flush. She looked away but she was sure Sarah and Phillip Moreland must have noticed. A large dog running around the corner saved her, however, as it jumped up on Benjamin with dirty paws.

'Down, Conan,' Sarah commanded but the dog took no notice at all, stepping over her husband to get to her.

By now they were all laughing at the muddy footprints everywhere and Willa decided she liked the Harcourts immensely. When the dog was under control Phillip asked Benjamin if this dog was a relative of the ones that used to be at Summerley Court.

'He certainly is. The great grandson of Fion, if you remember him. We have always had Irish Wolfhounds.'

So that is what this animal was, Willa thought. She'd never seen such a big dog close up but this one looked like an adolescent who only wanted to play. Tentatively, she held out her hand and a tongue came out to lick her fingers, much to her delight.

'How old is Conan?'

'Only ten months, which is why he is so unruly. But with training he will turn out to be a fine dog, Ben is sure of it.'

'On days like this I am less so,' her husband answered with humour. 'Shall we walk to the lake? It is a short stroll and then we could go in and have lunch.'

The sky was full of scudding clouds over blue and the breeze was gentle as they ambled down a green pathway cut through the long grass. The lake came into view quickly.

'Did you swim here when you were on holiday?' Willa asked the Earl, and he shook his head.

'Phillip never liked the water much even on the

hottest day.' Benjamin answered for him. 'I don't think you ever swam once here, did you?'

'No.'

She saw the tension in Phillip Moreland even as the others did not and for a moment she wondered at what sort of childhood he had had, the picture being built by Benjamin one of a boy who had been thin, ill-clothed and often injured.

That thought had her listening more carefully to the words beneath the words as Benjamin rattled on about their summer meanderings. The closeness they'd shared was obvious, but why had they not kept up their friendship after leaving school? Why had it been so difficult to come to Elmsworth Manor?

Perhaps Phillip Moreland held as many secrets as she did?

'Did you invite Benjamin back to Hampshire?' she asked the Earl as they ambled back up the path. This time they were walking together, the others slightly behind them.

'I didn't. My mother was often sick, so it was easier for my father to tend to her without having to worry about anyone extra.'

'Where did Oliver go?'

'To our father's old uncle and aunt in Bristol, but they could only ever deal with one child at a time, and so as the youngest he went. I was glad not to be chosen, as coming here to Summerley Court was far more fun.'

'Poor Oliver.'

He turned and looked at her.

'I never thought of it like that but I suppose it was difficult for him. After our mother died, he put his foot down and went to his own friends and I continued to holiday at Summerley.'

'How did she die?'

'She drowned.'

'Is that why you do not like to swim?'

'It's part of the reason.' He said no more.

Wilhelmina St Claire was putting all Benjamin Harcourt's confidences together and coming up with a picture of himself as a child, Phillip realised. He could see the pity in her eyes and he did not want that. He wished Benjamin would say no more about their history or their exploits. They still had to get through lunch and part of the afternoon before they could leave for London and the hours left worried him.

Why had he not thought of this? Wilhelmina was both clever and intuitive and he saw that she listened carefully to what was being said. He had not wanted to answer the question about his mother but it was difficult not to, so he had only given her a little of the answer.

The lake dark under the evening light and the water rough and deep, blood running down his arms and leg from where his mother had cut him with a knife and Oliver screaming from the upturned boat.

He felt the sweat bead on his forehead. This place brought back memories that he did not want to resurface.

'Where did you go for holidays as a young girl?' If he changed the subject it might be easier.

'Nowhere. Mama and Papa were always busy.'

'You had no siblings?'

She shook her head.

'No pets?'

'I did have a hedgehog that lived under a bush by the front door. I fed him until Papa tossed him into the stream because he was eating too many of the insects that they wanted to study.'

'Did they know you valued it?'

'Probably not. They weren't monsters, they were just extremely focused on their work, as I said.'

'How do children ever get through childhood in one piece?'

'I don't know,' she returned. 'Perhaps they do not, really.'

'Unless they have parents like Sarah and Ben and life is just a wonderful adventure?'

She nodded. 'And then they flourish.'

Such a truth was sobering but Phillip did not wish for melancholy to blight their day.

'It is so good to be out of the city, and this part of Richmond is gentle and green.'

'I thought your part of Hampshire was beautiful as well.'

'It is wilder, I think. Less civilized.'

'There is a charm in that, too,' she gave him back, and sounded as if she meant it.

'Where exactly is Belton Park?'

'It lies very close to Winchester, though in all truth we hardly ever ventured to the town.'

'Why not?'

'I told you before, everyone was busy with their work and I did not know anyone there.'

'You were not brought up in those parts?'

'No, I was born in the south, in Romsey. My parents met Lionel through their meetings with the scientific community, and when I was sixteen he invited our family for an extended stay at Belton Park.'

'Because he desired you as a bride?'

'Probably, but I did not know it then. If I had I would never have gone but by that time it was too late. My parents liked him and were happier than they had been for a long time, and I suppose I liked the cordiality and the sense of peace in the house and its grounds. So when he asked me to marry him I said yes without a second thought. Regret came a few months later.'

'So little time.'

'Well, I'd made the mistake and had to live with it, and my parents both died within a few months of each other about five years later.'

'So you were stuck?'

'I was stuck even before that because Mama and Papa would never have supported me should I have told them how unhappy I was with my marriage to Lionel.'

'So you said nothing?'

She turned to look at him. 'What could I have said? There could be no annulment by then and we had no other place left to go to anyway.'

'Fait accompli?'

She smiled. 'Exactly. Most people don't have a lot of choice. It was just that I made the wrong first choice and suffered because of it. You were luckier.'

'Luck has a certain habit, though, of running out.'

'Your wife's sickness, you mean?'

He didn't answer and was glad when she posed no more questions.

When they returned to the house Ben beckoned

them into the old library at the far end of the corridor.

'I thought you would want to see these, Phillip. They will certainly bring back memories.'

There before them were two boards detailing in words and drawings all the things they had done in the summer holidays at Summerley one year. The date was embellished with paint of all hues and their names were written underneath.

The jolt of being taken back to that time and seeing his teenage handwriting was staggering. 1803, a year after his mother had died and when he was struggling to survive himself.

'You were not at school at all that year and half of the one before, Phillip, but you came to us in early June and stayed till August. It was the best holiday I can remember because Mama always allowed anything we suggested, even the more outlandish activities.' He pointed to one of the squares. 'See, there is that tree hut we built and there is the fire we made? Remember the slingshots we fashioned and you shot that wild turkey and we took it home and the cook prepared it for dinner?'

'Good memories,' Phillip said but underneath he could only remember how he had struggled that summer, with sadness and with fear, all the emotions he had been careful to hide from Ben.

The boards were an echo of the time when everything had changed, his family unit, his father, his brother. It was the beginning of an ending that had been so complete. Every picture and caption on those boards was a reminder of an innocence that had been lost and had never again been found.

Wilhelmina was looking at him in a way that he had not seen her look before, and he turned away.

'I'm starving even thinking about that turkey,' he said, whereupon Sarah said lunch was ready and about to be served if they could all repair to the dining room.

The rest of the afternoon was easier, the talk about London nowadays and the balls that had occurred so far in the Season. Wilhelmina spoke of her life there, too, and her stories took away the focus from him.

At three o'clock the carriage was ready to depart and they gave their farewells, promising to get together again as soon as possible. As the carriage pulled away Philip took in a breath and closed his eyes, urging himself back into calm.

'You once asked me why I liked masked balls so much.' Her soft voice broke into his thoughts and he sat forward and looked at her as she explained.

'It was simply because everything was more distant and hidden. My mistakes. My family. My husband. I always felt safer when no one could see how much the past had hurt me.'

She had understood him exactly as he fought to get his emotions under control. He'd had no mask today but he had survived. A few years prior he would not have managed anywhere near as well.

He wondered if he should tell her some of what had happened to him but held back because such a confidence could also be a burden for her and he did not want to give her worries that were his to deal with. Gretel had done that to him, time and time again, and each confession had seemed more and more like a heavy anchor.

So instead he brought her fingers up and placed a soft kiss on the back of her hand before letting it go.

'Thank you for listening,' he said. 'Today would have been a lot more difficult without you there.'

Her smile was bright, the gold in her eyes catching a beam of sunlight that had slanted into the carriage at the turn of a bend.

Everything in her was centred on the man beside her, the feeling of connection strong.

Inside her heart beat faster, her breath was deeper and an odd feeling of heat crept through her body. Even the air around them contained something that was different, leaving her feeling light-headed and strange. Her reaction was ridiculous, she knew that it was, and she hoped that he would not notice her fluster.

'Benjamin and his wife are looking well.' His words were quiet. 'It was a coincidence that you and Sarah were acquainted.'

'It was.' Her smile felt as artificial as her reply.

'He said he would be in London next week on some business.'

'That is good.'

She did not want these nothing words, not with all that she was feeling.

He was quiet then as though he too had decided such a conversation was pointless, and the silence thundered between them until he spoke again.

'I was not happy as a boy.'

Better words. More real.

'I am sure you discerned that from Ben Harcourt's conversation. It was a difficult time for me.'

'Why?'

'Our family was struggling.'

She waited for more but the minutes lengthened.

'Most families struggle at some point.' She felt she needed to give something back. 'Mine certainly did.'

He looked at her then, his blue eyes silvered in an unexpected sadness. 'I have always admired your ability to say exactly the right thing at the right time, Wilhelmina.'

Her throat thickened as she held back tears at his compliment.

'I don't mean to make you sad, it's just I never realised that someone might hold a gift like that. My wife never had such a knack.'

A different truth and so unexpected. Everything she had seen or heard of the beautiful Miss Gretel Carmichael had placed her on an unassailable pedestal. The perfect woman and the perfect wife.

'If it makes you feel better, my husband would not have said the same of me, either.'

He smiled then and looked outside, the rows of trees close and blurred with the speed of the carriage. At their feet the bunch of colourful flowers from Sarah's garden was carefully laid down.

'You once asked me if I believed people might look at us from the afterlife and I replied that I hoped not. But I think I feel differently now because perhaps those who are gone and who did love us would have liked to see us happy.'

'People like your wife?'

'Yes.'

A kind answer and one that placed her questions about his relationship with Gretel at rest. Phillip Moreland had cared for her and if she had not perhaps filled all of his needs then she had still met enough.

'I will not marry again but sometimes…'

He stopped and looked at her, a hope in his eyes that could not be missed, and without thinking she simply leant forward and kissed him softly on the cheek, so that he could move away if he wanted to. She was a free and independent woman and had been since her husband died, but Phillip Moreland had awakened something in her that could not be ignored. When his hand curved around the back of her neck and he brought her closer she did not resist, and when he changed the angle of the kiss so that his mouth slanted across her own she asked for more. This was not like the kiss in the Elmsworth kitchen, but a fiercer, more desperate variety, and one that asked for things that had not seemed possible back then. She opened to him, inviting him in, feeling in the passion a different request, a more sensual one, a need that went beyond what was offered.

His mouth fell lower to her throat, his free hand moving across the rise of her breast. You are mine, every action seemed to say, mine in flesh and lust, in appetite and fever.

There was no reason left in her, no will to stop what was happening. She wanted to lie down on the seat and tear open her dress so that he could find the secrets of all that lay underneath and take them. But he was suddenly still and his words were a far cry from the thoughts she was having.

'Lord help me,' he said as he pulled her against him, his breath as ragged as her own. 'I cannot take you like this. It is wrong.'

Wrong because he did not want her? Wrong because he still loved his wife? Wrong because she had acted like a loose woman and it had shocked him?

She ground her teeth together and sat up very straight, for already the outskirts of London were visible through the window and she could not quite understand what might happen next.

'I am sorry.' His quiet apology only made her angry and she shook her head, for she did not want that from him. She had misjudged him, misjudged his needs and her own. If she could have left the carriage then and there she would have, but there was still a good twenty minutes before that would be possible, so they were stuck together in the silence of regret.

Wilhelmina collected her flowers and exited the conveyance as soon as it stopped, disappearing into her town house on Russell Square without once looking back.

'Damn,' Phillip whispered softly into the shadows

of the waning day. He had wanted to take her hand and explain what he'd meant by 'wrong' and if she had given him even one sign of desiring clarification he would have given it. But she had sat ramrod stiff against the seat, the fingers of her right hand twisting the silk in her skirt in a way that told of great agitation. He had not had much experience with the ways of women apart from his wife, and Gretel's anger at him at times seemed mirrored in Wilhelmina's posture.

Surely she understood why it would have been wrong? He could ruin her for one and she would be forever exiled if anyone were to observe them. It had to mean more, be more, on both of their parts, this binding of the flesh. It could not be a nothing thing decided in a second in a moving carriage on a public street.

The whole day had been a disappointment to her, no doubt, and perhaps after her own troubles she now did not have the heart to take on the wretched truths of another man who would only disappoint her further.

He could not blame her for that either but the hope of it left him empty. He didn't want to go home to the Moreland town house and at this hour of the evening he could not safely leave for Elmsworth Manor either.

The thought of his private club in the city came to mind, a place he had rarely visited but one which could now provide a drink and limited company. Banging on the carriage wall, he waited for the driver to slow before giving him new directions.

White's was just as he remembered it, with its green walls, red seats and blue carpet, and as he came to the set of steps leading to the second floor he did feel a comforting sense of familiarity.

The salons were far busier at this hour than he'd imagined they would be but he did not turn away, walking instead with intent to a table in the darker end of the first room and sitting on one of the expansive leather chairs beneath a window. The barkeep came before he could even look around and he remembered the stellar service of the place with a smile.

'Whisky, please.' The drink of broken men and their broken dreams. It seemed appropriate.

A number of the brands available were mentioned and he chose the last one, only because he had not really listened to the first options. Within a moment the man was back with a full glass, the bottle it had been poured from set beside it on a silver tray.

'Thank you.'

'It is our pleasure, Lord Elmsworth.'

Everywhere he went they knew his name. So unlike America, where he had journeyed alone. Lifting the glass, he finished it and then poured himself another. And another. The room began to feel less sharp, Wilhelmina's kiss a warming memory, and he liked how reality slid away into something else. Drink was how he had coped after Gretel's death, the way he had got himself up every morning and lived.

But tonight it felt different. Wilhelmina St Claire was a mile away in her Bloomsbury town house, readying herself for bed, untying her hair, slipping between the sheets, finding sleep.

He imagined her dreams, freedom probably as much a part of them as the awful ending of their late-afternoon carriage trip.

He stared into the space before him to try and find the thought that was eluding him, skimming on the edge of his reasoning. Then he had it. He wanted the same things as she did. Freedom and the space to be alone, and had she not told him time and time again that she wasn't a woman who gossiped?

He sat up straighter and helped himself to another whisky. The alcohol was giving him a clarity he had not had before, a way forward that might be conducive to them both if they were brave enough to try.

Not a replacement for Gretel, never that, but a woman whom he liked and admired. As permanent as she wanted it. Or as temporary. Private. Hidden.

Undisclosed. When Wilhelmina tired of him, which he knew would happen, they could simply say goodbye in a civil fashion, and get on with the rest of their lives.

Not a love story either, which stripped the guts from you and left you writhing from betrayal, but a logical, lucid and well-structured plan. A plan that no one, save them, ever needed to know of.

Could it work?

Was it possible?

How could one go about even suggesting it without sounding…arrogant? Society had called him that before he'd left, the Arrogant Earl, they had said and if he had heard it then she would have, too.

Attraction had its limitations but it also had its strengths, though he would need to be careful in his approach, for he did not want her to flee. It would take time, this courtship of the flesh. Smiling, he poured his sixth glass, the room swimming when he looked up, the rocking making everything unsteady under the glow of chandeliers attached to ornate coffered ceilings.

Was he drunk enough or too drunk? He replaced the cap on the bottle and sat back, reorganising his thoughts. It had been a long time since he had felt the full thrust of truly good whisky and it was having an effect.

'Is there something else you might require, my lord?' The same attendant was back a few moments later, his eyes taking in the empty glass and the capped bottle. 'Some food perhaps?'

'No. I am just leaving.'

'Have you a carriage in the vicinity, my lord? I could hail it if you would like?'

'I do not but it is fine.'

A deep frown marred the man's forehead. 'I should not advise walking alone, Lord Elmsworth, for there have been some nasty incidents in the last few months in this vicinity with footpads and the like.'

America had cured him forever of worrying about danger, and besides, the skills he had acquired from his solo travels were varied and many.

'I will keep that in mind but thank you for the warning.' Bringing a substantial sum from his pocket, he placed it on the table by the whisky. 'If you could find my hat and coat I would be grateful.'

'Certainly, my lord.'

Outside on St James Street Phillip breathed in the night air, enjoying the darkness and the silence. His town house was an easy walk away and he needed the exercise after so many sedentary days in London.

The first sign of trouble came five minutes later when two shadows passed in front of him at speed.

The stick that was brought down hard upon his head surprised him, though, for a third person he had not noticed before must have been hanging back. The whisky was making him careless, and he swore.

Balancing on his heels, he crouched low, his hat crushed on the street and the darkness more complete than he had expected it to be here in the city.

A good place for an ambush. No lights on in the buildings, no traffic on the road either. He caught the first assailant with a hard fist to the side of the head and he went down. The second one was faster, and a blow caught his own nose before he could trip him up and make sure that he stayed quiet. Two dealt with, then, and one to go. The third man held some sort of knife, for he saw the glint of the blade just before he felt the sharp cut of flesh on the rise of his cheek. When the miscreant came forward again Phillip ducked to one side and grabbed his hair, cracking his skull hard against the side of the brick building. The dropped knife turned and spun on the cobbles before stopping in the drain and then silence resumed.

Picking up his hat and rearranging his coat, Phillip walked on, glad for the lamp posts and the light as he turned a corner. There were people here now going home and the late-night street sellers still stood at their places.

'Spiced gingerbread to buy, milord, or hot baked apples?'

When he shook his head his nose ached and he touched it, seeing the blood on his fingers. He didn't think it was broken. In America he'd had his wrist and two of his fingers broken and they had hurt a hell of a lot more than this. His cheek would need stitches though, the skin gaping in a two-inch cut. But it was a comforting thought that the appearing street names were only minutes from his town house and the area he was in now was far more salubrious than the street he had just left.

There was an energy in a fight that banished all ennui, something he remembered from his months of anger on the road after Gretel had taken her last breath. Lifting his hand to wipe the hair back from his face, he saw that he was shaking badly and he swallowed the need to throw up on the side of the road.

A headache was building, too, and he felt cold, but he was nearly home and he could deal with these things when he was.

Willa hated him. She did. She hated the way he had kissed her so absolutely and then held her at bay, telling her all they had done was wrong and that he was sorry for it.

Sorry. Even the word made her livid. Lionel had said sorry after each and every lash-out with either his body or his words and then he had done the same again and again and again. A pattern of abuse. A reminder of her place. An easy way of keeping her in check and in line.

Well, she was free and would not ever be tied again to the poor manners of men who wanted one thing and then said another.

Phillip had disappointed her and that was the worst of it. She had turned into a harlot in a matter of seconds as soon as his mouth had slanted across hers, unstoppable and desperate. Even now her heart was beginning to beat faster at just the thought of his hand on her breast and his mouth at her throat.

She walked closer to the mirror to look again at the redness he'd left on her skin. The marks of ownership and possession. The tip of her index finger trailed across her lips and she leant back to try to bring again the feeling of his being there. Intimate and private, his tongue running over her skin as he finished, rough and warm and then cool against the air.

She hoped the heightened colour would not be able to be seen tomorrow above the edge of her gown, for it was such a particular thing. Everybody would know how it had got there, a lover's stain.

After so many years of her being numb.

She shook her head and walked to the window, looking out over the night. Two carriages were moving into the square and a young couple were meandering along the path by the park, caught up in each other's glance, oblivious to the whole world around them, their clothing meagre but their love grand.

She envied them and would have watched them further save for her maid coming into the room to help her undress and get ready for bed. Being careful to turn in a direction which would not lead to any discovery of the evidence of Phillip's ardour, Willa slipped her gown and petticoats off and then put her lawn nightdress on, glad for its volume and covering as the maid loosened her hair and brushed it out.

When she was finally alone she reached for the diary she kept by her bedside and sat on the chair at her small desk. Dipping the quill in a new bottle of ink, she began to write.

Chapter Eight

It was Tuesday and Willa had heard absolutely nothing from the Earl, receiving neither a note nor a visit. Had he returned to Hampshire, the awkward carriage journey from Richmond to London a catalyst to send him scurrying away from any interaction with her?

Phillip Moreland always defaulted to distance if the conversation became personal. He had shown his true self a few times, she amended, when she'd seen beneath the more normal veneer, but the raw truths of his life were quickly covered over by other means. He was indeed the master of disguise even outside of a masquerade ball. That thought made her frown further.

When Anna Cherton arrived for a visit half an hour later Wilhelmina knew by the excitement in her eyes that she had news.

'There is talk of Lord Elmsworth all over town,

Willa. It seems he has been in some sort of a fight and has black eyes and wounds, which explains his absence from events lately. Everyone has commented on it.'

'If he has been so out of Society, how would anyone know of his injuries?'

'His valet is the husband of one of my maid's daughters and you know how servants talk. Probably it is the fastest and the most accurate gossip-mill in town, if one thinks about it with all those connections just joining up the dots.'

'Do these rumours state where he was injured?'

'They do, indeed. Phillip Moreland was blind drunk when he arrived home at his town house late at night three days ago and as furious as his valet had ever seen him. It seems he was in a fight in a back-street tavern and he reeked of cheap whisky.' Anna gave her this gossip with a raised brow.

Wilhelmina counted back the days. Last Friday was the day they had gone to Richmond to see the Harcourts. Why had he then got so drunk he'd been in a fight? Nothing made sense to Wilhelmina. Perhaps the talk of his difficult childhood had left him angry? Or had their dreadful ride home made him irritated? Either way a man who could not control his emotions and one who got drunk on a whim was hardly stable.

That thought left her frowning.

'It seems his star might have fallen amongst the desperate mamas of Society looking for a suitable husband for their daughters, Willa, for there are other stories also circulating of Phillip Moreland's temper. I heard it implied today that he tried to kill his brother.'

Willa remembered George's words on this very same incident as she waited for Anna to explain.

'It apparently was about a year before he left for America and he has rarely been seen with Oliver Moreland in Society since.'

The shades of damage rose and in London that could be a dangerous thing indeed. Was this why he had not surfaced since? Or was he hurt far worse than anyone knew?

Wilhelmina breathed in to try and distil her worry and was pleased when Anna left soon afterwards.

She would send Phillip Moreland a note. She would not sit here and fuss. After Lionel she had promised to act upon her misgivings because she would never again allow herself to be left in a position of powerlessness. A short, crisp, to-the-point letter wondering how he fared would not be out of place, given their strange relationship, and it would set her mind at rest at the very least.

Phillip arrived in the early afternoon at her town house, his card brought into the day room by her butler.

'Please show the Earl in,' Wilhelmina said, glancing at her reflection in the mirror just to check everything was in order.

His face when he entered the room was much, much worse than Anna's tale had described it to be. Both eyes were swollen and damaged. His cheek held a substantial stitched cut and his lip was split at one corner, the abrasion flowing to his chin. The bruises across his nose were yellow, green and purple but the look in his eyes invited no sympathy at all from her.

'Mrs St Claire.' Formal, firm and direct.

'My lord,' she returned in the same vein, hating the way the blood rushed to her face.

'Thank you for your note. As you can see, I am still alive.'

'If barely,' she gave him back, and went straight to the crux of the matter. 'Rumour has it you were blind drunk on cheap whisky and itching for a fight in some back-street tavern.'

'The whisky part is almost correct, though it was certainly not cheap. My place of choice was actually White's, the private club I have belonged to for years and from which I elected to walk home. The fight part came after I was attacked on a particularly dark corner by three assailants I had never seen before and hopefully never will again.'

'A rather different story, then, to the one circulating? Why have you not thought to correct such discrepancies? Society at the moment is raking through your past history to find other misdemeanours and your currency in the marriage stakes has fallen markedly because of it all.'

'Well, that is at least one plus from all of this.'

His smile was crooked and so very beautiful that Willa turned away. 'Can I offer you a cup of tea and soft cakes? Or are even they going to be difficult to eat in your present condition?'

He ignored her banter. 'I would like that.'

'Then you should sit down,' she said next, calling her butler to give him the details of what they wished to eat and drink. 'Don't make the tea too hot,' she added at the end and saw him smile again.

'Three assailants seem quite a number, Lord Elmsworth.' Such formality would put him exactly in his place.

'Two were easy. It was the third one who mostly did this. He came at me with a knife.'

'My goodness.' She hated the tremble in her words.

'I should have listened to the barkeep at my club and heeded his warning of ordering a carriage, for there have been other recent attacks in the same area apparently. I had certainly imagined the amble home to be more peaceful than it turned out to be.'

'But you disposed of them anyway. Where did you learn to fight?'

'In America. I was not an earl there, you see. I was simply a broken-hearted widower who travelled in questionable company over many miles and months. One learns the lay of the land, so to speak.'

'Which is to attack or be attacked?'

'Exactly.'

'Then it would probably be conducive to your reputation to reappear in Society in an attempt to repair the damage.'

'I think I almost killed one of them.' Horror had her mouth opening. 'The man who taught me how to fight held no sway with allowing mercy.'

'I see.'

'Four years in the wilderness in a foreign land does nothing to temper forgiveness, either.'

'Did you also try to kill your brother?'

His gaze sharpened and she was glad for it.

'That is another of the stories now circulating which you would do well to know of.'

'No. I did not. I meant to miss.' He said no more even though she waited.

'Well,' she began finally when he did not speak, 'if you value your position here in Society at all you must attend the Kelland ball in five days and appear as if this has all been a truly dreadful mistake. Attacks come in different forms, my lord, and this one shall simply be subtler. I intend to be there, so I can help you in your quest for impunity.'

'You would do that for me? I thought after the carriage ride…'

She did not let him finish. 'The intimacy between us was unwise, my lord, but I am not a person who just turns aside when injustice is served up no matter who the injured party is or isn't.'

'Touché,' he gave her back and smiled. 'Though I might be construed as a poor candidate for restoration, given that my injuries will still be more than noticeable.'

'Think of them as a badge of being in the wrong place at the wrong time. Any one of the members of Society could be in that position, and they know it.'

'Lord.' He ran his left hand through his hair and she saw marks on all the knuckles. She also saw he no longer wore his wedding ring. God forbid the thieves had stolen it but she did not feel up to asking.

'Sometimes the struggle to fit back into London Society hardly seems worth it.' His words came after a moment or two.

'I understand that completely, my lord. But if you find it in you to quit the city altogether then it is far better to do so on your own terms.'

'You are ruthless, Mrs St Claire.'

'Almost as ruthless as you are, Lord Elmsworth, and I use it as a protection to never again be trampled under the feet of others.'

'"Though she be but little, she is fierce."'

'Helena from *A Midsummer Night's Dream*? You surprise me, my lord.'

'I could say the same of you, Willa.'

The first time he had addressed her so informally. A détente, born out of necessity. The kiss in the carriage shimmered between them under the words, slicing away reason, causing a stalemate.

When the cake and tea came the talk became more general but Willa missed the sharp and clever conversation from before.

Willa did consider not going altogether. She could still send an apology saying that she was ill or indisposed and yet here she was about to be dressed in the most beautiful gown she owned because tonight she had to appear as the sort of woman Phillip Moreland, the eighth Earl of Elmsworth, might genuinely choose to spend a dance or two with.

To run would lead to questions on his behalf and would incite more conjecture about her motives and so she bathed in lavender water and her maid fashioned her long hair into a soft style of tumbling curls. The dark blue dress she had donned was both sensual and classical and the small matching hat was cleverly fashioned.

She wore rings on her fingers and a necklace of diamonds at her throat and she allowed her maid to colour her lips and apply light blush to her cheeks.

'You look the most beautiful I have ever seen you appear, miss,' her lady's maid said when they both took in her image in the full-length mirror. And in all honesty Wilhelmina was inclined to agree. Her own taste was far more eclectic and out of step with the modern style. This gown, hairstyle and jewellery fitted in exactly, right down to the pale kid leather slippers on her feet.

She looked perfect. Money helped. Under the chandeliers her diamond necklace would sparkle and the material in both her gown and hat was of the finest Belgium lace.

Like the knights of old bedecked in their armour she was ready to do battle, though the small niggle of why worried her. Phillip Moreland was not one to be trifled with and yet he was the first man she had ever felt drawn towards. This feeling was inexplicable and foolish, given his reaction to their kiss, but it was none the less the truth. Taking in a breath, she made herself smile.

When she arrived at the Kellands' town house she saw the Earl exiting his carriage right behind her, surprise in his eyes as he took in her appearance, a message of appreciation darkening the blue. His own clothing was of an understated finery, a black jacket and trousers of thin wool and a white shirt with a necktie that was neither foppish nor insubstantial. The wounds on his face were remarkably recovered in the five days since she had seen him, the stitches removed from his cheek and his eyes much less swollen.

In his hand he held out a small bouquet of flowers, the fat, creamy buds nestled within the shiny green of a few leaves.

'The perfume you use is made up of gardenias and I thought you would enjoy these.'

'Thank you.' Such a genuine gift almost put the stamp of authenticity on their outing and she had to remind herself tonight this was just a ploy and a way to beat the Ton at their own game while simultaneously protecting the ancient title of Elmsworth. Tucking the floral tribute into the top fold of her small bag, she allowed him to lead her inside.

Like a fairy tale.

Like Cinderella finally going to her ball.

Except she did not wear glass slippers and her Prince Charming wanted very little to do with her.

Phillip understood the Ton as Wilhelmina did not. He knew of Society members' propensity to cut each other down in order to elevate themselves and he knew that his past arrogance would also count against him. On the surface there would be politeness but underneath a darker tone would linger. He hoped Wilhelmina might understand the reality of things, too.

She was beautiful, and that was a point in their favour. She was also very clever, which might not be so helpful, for the kingpins of Society had no wish to bow down to the intelligence of a woman who had neither elevated lineage nor family history on her side.

Mrs St Claire was a jigsaw puzzle and a far more formidable opponent than anybody here may have yet realised. It would be an interesting night ahead but she was right in her summation of his want to quit Society on his own terms, and although he had no love for the theatrics of the Ton he did not wish to be shoved off without choice either.

He liked the way she laid her hand on his arm as if she needed to be ready.

'This won't be easy.' He said this softly.

'Oh, I think we have both been through far worse.'

Joseph Kelland was the first to meet them. 'Elmsworth,' he said with an inflection of question. 'It seems you have been in the wars in more ways than one.' His glance then rested on Wilhelmina. 'Mrs St Claire.'

'Your house looks very beautiful tonight, my lord.'

A sincere compliment which made Kelland smile as he brought his wife forward. 'Mrs St Claire was just saying how lovely the house appeared, my dear, and as it is mostly your doing I thought you should be the one to hear it first.'

'You are more than kind.'

As she went on to describe to Wilhelmina the details of getting everything ready Joseph Kelland pulled him aside.

'I did not think you would make an appearance tonight, Elmsworth. There are whispers all over Society about your poor behaviour and those of good sense and conservative values are not pleased.'

'Which is why I am here to state my side of things.'

'Indeed, and you are right to come and stand your ground but I am warning you because some might not be eager to listen.'

'I shall be careful. I hope my presence here will not cause problems for you.'

'Oh, do not worry on my account. Society is boring me to death of late so at least this evening might be a more interesting one than most.'

They'd moved away from the reception line into the body of the main room now and Phillip could hear whispers around them, Oliver's name mentioned more than once. That was the incident he could not refute and he wouldn't either, for the shame of his actions still hung in every part of him.

Catching Wilhelmina's anxiety, he tried to alleviate it.

'We shall slay them one by one. Just wait and see.'

'Like dragons?'

They both smiled as a Society doyen glided over looking a little like one.

'You have been in the wars, Elmsworth. It is the talk of the town.'

'Leaving White's early in the evening is a dangerous past-time these days, Lady Kensington.'

'I do believe you are right. I have said to my husband there should be more constabulary on the streets but the city is too poor to afford them.' She turned then to Wilhelmina.

'You are looking remarkably well tonight, Mrs St Claire. A lack of feathers and your hair down suits you. Have you changed your lady's maid?'

A backhanded compliment delivered with perfect timing, Phillip thought, and saw a spark of irritation in Wilhelmina's eyes.

When the woman's husband and sister-in-law also joined them the conversation included the mention of Oliver's name and he knew what was coming next.

'Have you seen your brother since you have returned?' Lord Kensington asked this.

'I have. His estate lies only thirty minutes from my own.'

'A cordial visit, then? We had heard things have been more than difficult between you. I hope you left your hand-piece at home this time.'

The gloves were off, just as he'd known they would be. Kensington was not a man to beat around the bush.

'I think family matters are better left discussed by the family. My brother would probably feel the same.'

Wilhelmina now joined the conversation. 'I know Esther and Oliver were hoping you might return last Christmas, Lord Elmsworth. I heard that they were most disappointed when you did not arrive.'

'Well, I am back now and I hope this year we might celebrate the season together.'

'It's such a lovely time, isn't it? I remember as a child in Winchester my father would find pine boughs and bring them inside, and the smell was so memorable. We would scour the woods around the town to find the greenest, freshest specimen and he would make sure I knew all the names of the insects we found on the branches.'

Phillip wondered at her great stream of words but

he knew what she was doing; shifting attention and calming the waters. Lord Holland and his wife ambled over next, even as Kensington continued his criticism.

'Your father would be turning in his grave at the way you are behaving, Elmsworth. If the mores of Society are not upheld in the best way possible the whole thing will collapse, you do realise that?'

'Oh, indeed I do, but I doubt the footpads outside of White's have heard that message.'

'You were at White's before you were attacked?' Lord Alfred Holland asked this.

'I was. The barkeep had warned me before I left of recent worrying incidents but I had no idea how brazen an attack might be.'

'Then I am glad to hear you fought them off. Perhaps a turn at a London boxing studio might not go amiss?'

'I will keep that in mind.'

Others listening in began to look less alarmed and angry and Phillip was grateful knowing that it only took a few moments for gossip to circulate in a Society ballroom. Already he could see a change in the mood.

When Ben and Sarah Harcourt and the Duggans joined them it all became easier again, being a group of people who buffered them, in a sense, from the others. Could it really be this simple? Taking a sip of wine, Phillip smiled at Lady Duggan standing nearby.

'When my niece had problems after the dissolution of her first engagement it was your brother who stepped in and rescued her, Lord Elmsworth.' Her words were quiet. 'Everyone needs a saviour now and then. Even you, I suspect. As Esther is my treasured niece, I consider you as part of my family and I was most pleased to see you at our masquerade ball the other week. You came as Hades, did you not?'

'The Lord of the Underworld seemed an appropriate disguise, Lady Duggan. My father's ceramic mask obviously did not fool you.'

'You have the old Earl's height and your mother's beauty. It was easy for me to see the man beneath.'

Astonished, Phillip kept silent. He could not remember that about his mother but this small truth was welcomed.

'Oliver has it, too. The same fineness. Miranda was a friend of mine at school and she would have been proud of you both had she been here today.'

He bit down on a reply, given all that had happened between him and his mother, but Lady Duggan was not yet finished.

'Second chances are not for the faint of heart,

though I have always been of the mind everyone deserves to fashion their own course in life.'

Willa had said as much to him. And Gretel on her deathbed had made him promise that he would go home to England and be happy. Could such a choice be possible? Even with his questionable reputation he felt hopeful, an emotion so unfamiliar it stunned him.

'Thank you, Lady Duggan.'

'You are welcome.'

Wilhelmina was next to him now. She had been prickly with him all evening but at least she had stuck to her word and helped him navigate the rumours.

'Tonight is turning out just as we hoped it would.' He said this softly to her and meant it.

'Bearding the lion in its lair has its advantages, and the sooner you do so the less the rumours escalate.' She looked directly at him.

'Are you speaking from experience?'

'I am. When I first arrived in London there were many tales that were not exactly favourable about me. But I learnt that hiding makes everything so much worse because imagination is limitless.'

'I cannot imagine you hiding from anything, Wilhelmina.'

He felt her shock and saw the rush of questions.

* * *

She was breathless, here in the room full of others, here with him before her with his cut face and bruised eyes. Despite their differences she wanted to touch those wounds, to simply reach out and wipe away all of his hurt, to feel his warmth against her fingers, and to see him smile.

She could not believe the strength of such a want either, after his insults of the other day and their distance ever since.

'Will you dance with me?'

She was unsure if she should, her body like a tuning fork vibrating to his words. Surely if he touched her he would feel it too? But she could not refuse without looking churlish.

She was thankful for her gloves as she laid her fingers against his arm and he led her to the floor, past those who watched them, past the gossip. She knew she was not a young girl of the first water, her age and looks counting against her, but tonight she felt beautiful, in her deep blue dress and partnered by a man who was unmatched in all of London's Society.

Her moment. Here and now. She would not diminish it and when the music began she faced him in the waltz.

He held her close, his movements small and careful, as if he were counting the steps so that he made no mistake.

'I seldom came to balls,' he confessed after a moment or so. 'Gretel never liked them and I was such a poor dancer I was pleased that she didn't.'

'I think you are doing well.'

He smiled. 'Now I know that you lie.'

'Well, a competent dance partner was never at the top of any list of mine.'

'What was at the top of your list?'

'Kindness. Strength. Honesty. Delight.'

'A varied menu?'

He brought her in, an action which chased away amusement. Had he meant to do that or was she imagining it?

But sometimes words were not needed at all. Sometimes spaces and heartbeats and breaths were all that were required to pass through the world. She imagined that she was standing at some sort of threshold in her life, a place of change should she choose it, a simple movement of consent, an invitation for more, a quiet, invisible sanction to all that might come after.

He'd said that he could not imagine her hiding from anything but she did hide her reaction towards him. She hid both disappointment and desire.

If she did not come straight to the point she knew

she was lost. Her fingers tightened across his and he looked at her, a question burning in the blue.

'I am going to be thirty-one this year, my lord. I would like to know "delight" before I get to the age of no return. I have no expectations of more.'

'Delight?'

'When you kissed me in the carriage the other day I did not think it was wrong.'

There, she had said it, here in a public room full of others under the light of the chandeliers, but she would not take it back.

'Lord.'

The hardness of the word was also translated into his body, stiff against her own, and even through the material of his jacket she could feel his heart-beat pounding.

'I do not expect you to change your mind, Lord Elmsworth. I am just giving you my point of view.'

He grimaced and it looked nothing like a happy gesture as he turned her in the dance, the music playing, the noise of talking, the turning colour wheel of dresses, the sounds of gaiety.

He could not believe she had just said that, here in this crowded ballroom. He wanted to take her hand and lead her away, out to his carriage, where they could talk properly and he could show her that he did not think that a kiss was wrong either.

But they were stuck here, glued to this charade, and he could not be seen leaving with her alone when every single eye was upon them. Surely she understood that?

'I agree with your point of view. I did not think it was wrong either.'

He said the words without looking at her, keeping the tone of them even, willing his body not to react in the way that it was wanting to. It was as though they were dancing in the middle of nothing, borne on only feeling, their bodies cocooning them in, and shutting every other single thing out.

He'd never known this with Gretel, this lustfulness, this sizzling sensual tension that had nothing to do with being in love. He'd always been so measured, so restrained, so careful to keep his distance. It was the one certain thing he knew about himself.

'Can you define what you mean by delight?' His voice was husky.

'I have never had sexual relations outside of a small bedroom in the darkness with my husband. I have always kept my nightclothes on and I have never enjoyed it.'

His eyes widened this time but she kept going.

'Lionel thought the sins of the flesh were just that

and once he knew I could not produce children he lost interest completely, which suited me, though three days after Lionel died I did have one short and foolish dalliance with a man I trusted. I think I was not of a sound mind and it was dreadful and never again repeated.'

'So there was no "delight?"'

'No.'

'But you would like it?'

'I think with you I would.'

The music was coming to an end now and he carefully guided her over to one side of the room where they were sheltered by a pillar draped in tangled greenery.

Reaching over for two glasses of wine carried on a silver tray by a passing servant, he handed her one.

'What of the repercussions of this choice? Things like ruin or scandal?'

'I told you I don't want marriage ever again, but if we were careful in our relations, who would truly need to know?' She took a long sip of wine and then another one. 'As for scandal, well, I don't want to walk into old age unfulfilled even more than I don't want to be ruined.'

At this logic he laughed because right then and there he saw the utter magic in Wilhelmina St Claire. She was so unlike anyone else he had ever met, and though he had always seen hints of it, tonight the alchemy was fully present. She was not afraid of life or choice or passion and she had let him know it.

He felt his own character questioned under her onslaught of bravery, the shame of his words in the carriage the other day in such opposition to her boldness. It intrigued him, such a trait. A woman who could take on all the world and win.

Less brave women had always defined his life. Both Gretel and his mother had been melancholic women and they had dragged him down with them even if they had not meant to. He was turning thirty-three next birthday, and he was unfulfilled. In that way Willa and he were very alike.

He also knew that he had made a mistake on the trip back to London the other day with his words and so now he was much more careful.

'I am not Lionel, Wilhelmina. I can at least promise you that. I am also not looking for a quick dalliance that means nothing.'

He could not touch her, not here, he could not feel the racing pulse at her throat or trace the outline of her lips. He could not kiss her but he could make a promise and he could keep it.

'Thank you.' Her simple words spoke volumes.

Bringing his glass up, he clinked it against her own, but as he drank he adjusted the fit of his trousers by moving slightly, because if his words were measured his body's reaction was not. He felt eighteen again and in the first flush of sexual desire when everything was possible and nothing was out of the question.

And yet everything was. Marriage. Love. A future.

When the music stopped Miss Arabella Montague came over to them.

'Next week I shall be departing for France, Lord Elmsworth, for a sojourn to the south coast. As I am away for a few months I hope I may even venture into the north of Italy. Have you been there?'

'I went to Paris once a long time ago.' Phillip noticed how she ignored Wilhelmina. 'But in fact, my travels around Europe have been very minimal.'

'Florence is a city I have seen a great many drawings of and to simply walk through the arches of the Piazza Della Signoria or across the Arno to the Palazzo Vecchio seems like a dream. But I suppose you felt that way, too, about some of the American cities with their architecture and landscapes.'

'I did.'

He kept his answer concise because he could see Willa getting ready to walk away and, short of reaching out to keep her beside him, he could do nothing to stop her departure. When Arabella laid her hand across his arm he knew escape was going to be difficult.

'I am sorry for your troubles the other night, my lord. I have heard it all over the ballroom that it was footpads who waylaid you outside White's and it makes me wonder what on earth is happening. Is nowhere truly safe?'

'It seems not, Miss Montague, so I would advise even more care in the streets of foreign cities.'

She frowned at those words and Phillip hoped that might mean she would move away. Instead she leaned forward. 'Would it be too forward of me to ask you for the next dance, Lord Elmsworth?'

Her smile was genuine and she looked very young, and besides, Wilhelmina had already gone, swallowed up by the sea of other guests.

'Of course, Miss Montague.' There was nothing else he could do without causing question.

Phillip Moreland was leading Miss Arabella Montague out onto the floor and the quick anger that arose in her was very soon replaced by another thought. Any gossip about his injuries was only one side of this evening. People may have noticed her and the Earl dancing together at the various balls over the past weeks and it was important to allay any lingering public question about their relationship if she wanted the privacy she hoped for.

She was a free agent and so was he. They had no demands from outside sources or prior agreements but she did not wish for the extra attention that Society pressure might bring.

She had been honest and he had been, too. Much more honest than any other person in her life had ever been. There was strength to be had in that and also pleasure. She would not be ashamed but she was also exhausted from the whole evening.

She wanted to be home, away from prying eyes and measured words. Away from truly beautiful young women as well with their unblemished pasts and dazzling futures. This was Phillip Moreland's world and she had no claim on anything more than the shared delight they had spoken of.

She went to find her hosts to say goodnight, the small, fragrant bunch of gardenias tightly clutched in her hand.

Chapter Nine

The following morning Phillip sent a note to Wilhelmina asking if he could call upon her after the noon hour. Receiving a reply in the affirmative, he then sat at his desk in the library trying to think of what he might say to her.

Just past the hour of one he was ushered again into her blue salon in Russell Square and by the same butler he had met a few days prior. He was pleased the house seemed quiet and that the servants he had caught sight of on his first visit were nowhere to be seen today.

She was standing by the mantel dressed in a white gown decorated with small blue sprigs of flowers. Her hair was bound in a loose way and fashioned low on the back of her neck.

When he shut the door behind them he felt like Eros, the trickster God of carnal love and sensuality. She looked nervous, so he came straight to the point.

'I would never hurt you. I hope you know that.'

She nodded but he could see caution in her eyes.

'I will never lie to you, either.'

She was magnificent standing before him. A woman who on her own terms had come to this moment without pretence or deception. He could only give such courage back.

'There is a lot about me that you do not know, Willa, but I think you also keep your secrets close. Sometimes that is all one can do to be able to live and I shall not ask you for those confidences. But what we do need is the truth between us from now on. Is that something you might agree to?'

'Yes.'

Thank God they were older, he thought then, and that they had both been married.

He did not offer love or falsities but he did offer himself and perhaps that was enough. In time they might tell each other things that could wrench them apart but for now he would keep it simple.

A contract of the body perhaps? It felt more attainable. It felt possible with the shimmering feeling of last night's confession of 'delight' hovering around them.

He was pleased the door had been shut by the butler after he left the room, for such privacy was welcomed. Moving forward, he gently rested one hand against the curve of her neck, feeling the pulse and measuring its quickness.

'We shall do only what you want, and at the speed that you want it. If you ask me to stop, I will.'

Still she did not look at him and the pink already in her cheeks had now flared to crimson. Tipping up her chin, he made her see him, the gold in her eyes sharp with something he did not recognise.

His brave and bold warrior woman was shaking in her boots.

His thumb rested on the beat of her heart in her throat. She knew it would be racing…she knew there was nothing she could do to hide her fear, which was not ideal. She needed him to pull her towards him without thought or word or question. She wanted her part in the whole thing nullified because she had no notion as to even where to begin.

She hoped he might stay silent, the language of the body kinder than the alternative. She did not seek sense or promises or logic. She wished it was night-time with the darkness covering all that she did not want to show him. She worried about the scars on her thigh and the gash on the shin, improperly healed after it had festered. She was nothing like his perfect, beautiful dead wife Gretel or any of the other stellar lovers a man like him must have known before he married.

He stepped forward now, his eyes not leaving hers. He did not speak. He only looked as his hand moved up to her cheek, his fingers fanning out and drawing her in. And then his mouth came across hers, opened and seeking, soft and questioning.

She felt him move so that he could be closer still, to taste her, to know her, to let her understand in such a kiss there should not be fear but only delight.

It was his gift to her and she took it.

Worry was abandoned for this moment and at this time he was hers, the heat of lust taking over. A new woman and an unrecognisable one, she wanted everything he might teach her and more. Tipping back her head, she opened to him further, the echo in her body making her breath come faster and her need grow stronger.

And if Lionel had always been selfish, Phillip Moreland was not. His other hand cradled the back of her head as he lowered his mouth to her neck and the skin above the lace in the bodice of the gown, and her breath simply held as she understood for the first time in all her life that she was not the empty woman she had been told she was but a sensual and responsive one, wanting more, aching for it.

Her fingers ran through his hair, feeling the length

of the darkness and pulling him closer, and when his teeth skimmed the top of her breast, she could no longer control anything she felt.

She hoped he might lay her down on the carpet to take her hard and fast, so that she had no way to make it wrong, no misstep or blunder. But he was only gentle as he edged away the soft material and released one breast. She felt her nipple tighten in pleasure and tighten again as his mouth covered her, sucking and lathing, every nerve in her body centred on the movement. Hers. To keep. To feel. To know.

She shook with the craving of it and with the waves that came, releasing every uncertainty written in her bones and understanding finally that a woman's body could be played like an instrument of music by a maestro who would take the time and care to do it.

She burst into tears then, large sobs of thankfulness, her breath uneven, the echoes of passion inside still very much present as she buried her face into the fine wool of his jacket. His arms came around her as she cried, trying to regain some composure. When she felt she might cope she took in a deep breath and moved back a step and he let her go without comment.

'I did not expect a kiss would be like that.' It was all she could say.

'It usually isn't,' he gave back, his words honest.

'I am not perfect…' she began but one finger came across her lips to stop her.

'To me you are.'

'I've never felt much before when…'

He stopped her. 'I know. You told me.'

'But I've wanted to.'

He smiled.

'Have dinner with me tonight at my town house, Willa.'

So much more was implied in his words and she was grateful. He would not rush. He would not spoil the anticipation. She had waited years for this, wanted to savour all that he might show her, and it seemed he understood. She had been wrong to wish it over so quickly and to negate her own part in it.

'I would like that.'

He bowed slightly and moved towards the door.

'Then I will send a carriage for you just before eight.'

As she nodded he left, closing the door behind him. Even that courtesy was appreciated because it gave her time to put herself together, and one glance in the mirror showed her the extent of her dishevelment.

Was this what delight looked like on a woman, the flushed cheeks and lips that were suddenly more full? Her eyes looked different too, the gold in them far more noticeable and languid. With care she re-bound the tendrils fallen from her chignon and read-justed the line of her bodice. She'd seen the paintings of Delaroche and Reubens and the Arcadian plea-sures of the Rococo paintings in the forbidden books the McAllistair sisters held dear from their father's collections, images where the viewer was invited to gaze voyeuristically upon the sleeping nymphs and pleading lovers. She'd never quite understood the allure until now, when the possibility of abandon-ment and relinquishment of her own sexual being was so very close.

Tonight after dinner. In the darkness. Away from this house. Glancing at the clock on the far wall, she counted down the hours. Six and a half hours. Four hundred and fifty minutes. Her hand pressed against her stomach to try to stop the growing need there and she rocked back and forth.

Delight. It was going to be hers. And she would take it without question.

Half an hour later the doorbell chimed again and for a moment she wondered if Phillip Moreland was back to rescind his promises and retract his invita-tion to dinner.

But the aristocratic diction of the McAllistair sisters was suddenly audible, and within a moment they were ushered into the salon.

Miss Jean, the oldest sister, spoke first, a tumbling torrent of words, each more unbelievable than the one before it.

'We are leaving London, dearest Willa, and you shall be the first to know of it. Our father's cousin's son has claimed the London house and the estate to the west and in a show of good grace has bequeathed us a beautiful cottage in Royal Tunbridge Wells with a garden and a stream and trees all around. It is just too good of an opportunity to pass up and of late we have found London dreary, cold and busy.'

'So we will travel down next week as the place is furnished already and there shan't be a thing to do to get it ready.' Christine added this as her sister stopped, her face full of joy. Even the least talkative sister, Mildred, seemed charmed by the change in their circumstances.

'Our second cousin has left two of his staff to see to our needs, a cook and a butler, and so if we take Genevieve with us as our lady's maid we will be all set up. Our benefactor has arranged accounts at the local shops as well and asked for all of our expenses to be passed on to him. I know it is a quick turn in direction but we have made our minds up to do it and at our age such an offer is not to be turned away. One must take risks sometimes, do you not agree?'

'Oh, I do. Truly.' Wilhelmina had found her voice amidst the excitement, though she knew she would miss these three dear old ladies when they left. They were eccentric and interesting and had been supportive of her since the moment she'd met them. 'You must give me your new address and I shall journey down to see you as soon as you send word that you are settled and receiving company.'

'Which is exactly what we thought you might say,' Jean began and, pulling an envelope from her bag, she laid it on the table. 'It is all here, my dear. The direction, the description and a short list of all the sights you might take in on the way down to us.' She suddenly stopped. 'You know, Wilhelmina, you are looking more beautiful today than I have ever seen you look. Perhaps finally your husband's hold on you is loosening and you are allowing life to flow in again?'

'We have heard you allotted Mr Phillip Moreland a dance or two at the Kellands' ball last night?' Christine said this. 'And I must say that the small opportunity we had of meeting him at Elmsworth Manor when you were so very sick did impress us.'

'We knew his grandparents, of course, and his father. The wife was more of a puzzle, for, while she was decidedly beautiful, she was also distant, and then she died extremely young.'

'The Elmsworths have had their tragedies, that is for sure, but then, what ancient family has not? It seems betrayals and early deaths live in the blood of the aristocracy and show themselves in every generation.' Mildred continued in the same vein, her frown heavy before she began to laugh. 'But there are advantages, I think, in all the material boons of collections, paintings and books that have been gathered through the ages.'

Willa had to smile, given her earlier thoughts of the erotic collection of prints the old women had shown her in almost the first week of meeting them. She wondered what might happen to those in the upending of the McAllistair sisters' living quarters.

But the time was ticking on and, although it seemed rude not to offer them tea and cakes, she really did have so little of it to spare before…

At that she stopped.

Her denouement? Her rebirth? Her delight?

Mildred saved her from saying anything when she suddenly stood, reminding her two other sisters of all they had to accomplish today and tomorrow and in the next week before they were whipped away south in a carriage to the town of Royal Tunbridge Wells and to another life.

Within ten minutes they were gone.

* * *

Phillip had given his servants and his cook the night off. He did not want others here when Wilhelmina arrived, for the assignation was fraught enough as it was without involving extra players.

He had sent his carriage to collect her too, reasoning that it would be less obvious. He held no insignia on his conveyance and was glad of it, for he wanted to protect her as much as he was able from the ever-prying eyes of others.

When he heard the doorbell ring he walked across the foyer and opened it.

'My lord.' Her words were soft as she removed her hat and coat, and he hung them on the stand near the door. Tonight she was wearing an emerald-green silk gown, her hair loosely caught as it fell long down her back. The silk suited his intentions, as it was fastened at the front with only very few buttons, the neckline low and unfussy.

She didn't appear as nervous as she had been this morning as he led her through to the dining room, the table set up already with a variety of cold meats, breads and warm vegetables beneath silver hoods.

'The cook prepared a meal before she left.'

'It looks tasty.'

As tasty as she was in the silk beneath the candles, her skin glowing and the slender column of her neck on show.

She was glancing around at the ancient family portraits on the walls now which were interspersed with landscapes of the Elmsworth estate through the different seasons. The colours were dark and sombre, he thought as he interpreted it all through her eyes; a room that caught the tones of his childhood and all of the loneliness there.

'If paintings could talk, what stories these might tell,' she said and smiled. 'My parents had no interest in their ancestors, so it is lovely to observe all yours.'

A different way of seeing it all, then, but he was glad there was not a portrait of himself and Gretel on display. Crossing the room to find two glasses, he filled them with brandy. After he handed one to her he held his own up.

'To us.'

He clinked his against hers even as he wondered just what that meant. Us? They had made no promises and demanded nothing from each other that might constitute a future. It was simply now. This moment. This night.

She wore no jewellery at all. Nothing she might leave here, no careless bauble that could be found and commented on. Nothing to trace what might happen between them. His body stiffened at the thought. He felt as much of a virgin as she probably did, years of celibacy, and now this.

He could not think of Gretel, either, because today he wanted her somewhere else, in a space that he did not inhabit. The freedom from his past made everything even sweeter as Willa's perfume filled the space like an elixir. Gardenias and traces of violets.

'I have it on good authority that my presence at the Kellands' ball last night has dampened all rumours about me. I shall not be hounded from London, after all, and I have you to thank for making me at least turn up and not surrender by retreating to Elmsworth.'

'I can't really imagine you doing that.'

'Oh, you might be surprised. People have often disappointed me.'

'I know that feeling well.' She made an effort to keep the anger from her words, given their present situation, for she did not wish the promise of delight to be reduced by a poor mood. No, she wanted everything he might show her about the pleasures of the flesh and the excitement of more. She shivered with the thought of it.

He led her over to the table and saw her seated. Then he took up his own place opposite. The light from the candles brought out the many shades in her hair, caramels, browns and chocolates. He loved the depths of her, the golden eyes and the gold too in her skin, a woman of contrast and aliveness. The rise of her breasts was easily seen over her decolletage. More temptation.

She was quieter tonight, her quick-fire wit buried beneath silence, and, picking up a plate, he offered her a selection of the meats. She took a few of the slices and watched him do the same. Then he removed the heated silver hoods and laid out the stuffed potatoes, threaded beans and caramelised carrots. Another board held warm freshly baked bread and softly whipped butter.

He had asked the cook to prepare a meal that could be placed on the table before they ate and he'd wanted a menu that was simple. This fare was exactly what he had ordered but he could barely taste it, other thoughts so much closer than food.

'My friends the McAllistair sisters, whom you met at Elmsworth Manor, visited me today. They are shifting south to live.'

Ordinary words. He shook his head to concentrate and gave her an answer.

'It will be warmer at least.'

'I think the London house has become too big for them, but they have so many things that they will have to leave behind here it seems a shame.'

'The world turns, I suppose, and people have to adapt.' As he was trying to. Her lips were full and so very kissable.

'Yet there are times when I wish it might simply stop.'

Did she mean now? He looked up. The piece of lamb he was chewing became drier and he swilled it down with the brandy. Perhaps he should have waited to eat until after the 'delight' but that seemed so calculated and deliberate somehow he had not thought to suggest it.

He didn't want to frighten her or rush her, that was the problem. But she, too, had put her eating utensils down and wiped her mouth with a napkin, her tongue running over her top lip.

Fire coursed through him as he caught her glance and then he was standing next to her, helping her to do the same, taking her hand and laying a kiss in her palm.

'I want you, Wilhelmina.'

He could no longer pretend interest in ordinary conversation or food.

'Then show me, Phillip.'

He kissed her gently, with no force in it, laying his forehead against hers as he finished, trying to take stock of what next might happen. And then she kissed him back, her hand on his cheek pulling him in, demanding more. She nipped at his lip, her tongue coming over the spot, showing him in her actions she did not want too much caution.

All restraint in him escaped and he leant in to undo the buttons on her gown, one by one by one, the billowing layers of green silk slipping down easily from her body and pooling around her feet as she stepped away from it.

Before him stood a goddess in a sheer lawn petticoat, garters of lace around the tops of her stockings and absolutely nothing else. No stays. No drawers, no concealing shift.

'I dressed for the occasion,' she whispered and he had to laugh because there was always this juxtaposition with her every time they had talked, this quickness and this humour.

'And I appreciate it.'

With care he bent to pull the garters threaded with white ribbon from her thighs and with them the sheer pale cream silk of her stockings. There was only the petticoat left now but her hands came up to indicate she would like this to remain, her nipples hard buds against such sheerness, rose pink under the gauziness of lawn.

Her body held curves in every place that it should, her breasts, her hips, the roundness of her stomach. She reminded him of the sirens in the paintings that he had seen in Paris on a trip taken a year or so before he'd married Gretel. Erotic, splendid paintings of the sensual form. He had never forgotten them.

She watched him closely, reading his expression, a smile in each corner of her lips. She knew how beautiful she was and did not try to hide it. She stood there in all her glory and lifted her chin.

'My husband was never pleased with my body shape.'

'Was he blind?'

'He liked thinner woman. He thought I was licentious. That was a word he used and I had to look it up to find out the meaning.'

'Sexually unrestrained?'

'No, not that. He would certainly not have liked that. I think he leant more to the other side of the word. He did not wish for me to tempt men, is what he said, and made me dress in clothes that were several sizes too big. He said that my body was lewd and that many would find it offensive.'

'Hardly.'

His hand reached to one breast and he stroked the fullness of it before his fingers fell lower to the curve of her waist and then the shapeliness of her hip.

'I have scars on my left leg. You have not yet seen those but if I tell you now they will not be such a surprise.'

'Do you really think I would care?'

She pulled up her petticoat and he looked because she seemed to want him to.

'How did it happen?'

'My husband's telescope fell.' Words under words. Lionel St Claire had been a bastard. Everything she said made that fact truer.

One hand came across his arm, the small, well-kept nails, unadorned fingers, and smooth skin.

'You are safe here, Wilhelmina.'

'I know.'

Removing his jacket, he loosened his necktie and disposed of that as well. He was a good five inches taller than her and he could see down the front of her petticoat, everything showing. With care he lifted up a strap and pushed it down over her arm, his mouth falling to her nipple, claiming the largesse and sucking hard.

She took in a breath, quivering in surprise. Earlier he had been tentative but tonight he was not. He wanted her to understand the power of sex, not the shame. His other hand moved down, hiking up the lawn. Finding the warmth between her thighs, he stopped. She looked at him then, her golden eyes challenging, her heartbeat faster, the sheen on her skin of pure, damp want.

'This is your centre.' He thought she needed the

words. 'This is where women rule men. This is the place of a woman's potency and a man's privilege.'

She opened her legs and invited him in.

But not yet.

Moving her back against the wall, he knelt and placed his mouth where his finger had been, tasting the sweetness, lathing his tongue up into the folds, finding her, finding himself. Softly and without force. It was a quiet path to ecstasy, not a blunt one. Any wrong move now and she would stop him. She was like a yearling learning to be broken in.

The minutes lengthened and her fingers clawed into his hair, a growing rigidity in her body, the slick wetness telling him what she needed. One moment or two and he would have her, ripe like a summer fruit. Readied.

He was driving her to madness, every part of her body reaching for that place where nothing mattered, where the room fell away behind tightly shut eyes as she concentrated on what her body was saying. More. More. More. Further. Harder.

And then gone.

She opened her eyes in surprise, breathing fast, barely able to speak, not wanting the end, the slither of red-hot feeling in the pit of her stomach unwilling to let go of what she had been so near to finding.

Delight. Why would he stop? Was that it? Was there not more?

He stood and lifted her easily into his arms and laid her down on the thickly tufted rug in the salon next door, a green room of little furniture but with long curtained windows down one whole side. Stepping back, he removed his shoes and trousers.

The shock of seeing him like that sent shivers of surprise through her. Lionel had looked nothing like Phillip Moreland. He'd been a man with red hair, a fat belly and skinny legs, and his private parts had reflected those characteristics.

Phillip Moreland on the other hand was like an Italian marbled statue and all in perfect proportion, so much proportion in fact she wondered if they would even fit together. That thought made her breathing deeper, because there was a certain anticipation that could not be denied within it.

As he knelt he took her hand and allowed her to feel him, his hardness and his length. The candles burned in their sconces above this makeshift bed; there were no blankets, no closed doors either. It was as if he had fashioned a tryst, with all of her needs for delight furnished. She would not be able to hide and he would let her discover him without shame. An open, honest pleasure with no time limit, the whole night before them in his empty house.

As he came down beside her she felt the warmth of his body fully along hers, his hands bringing her face to his as he kissed her, more quickly this time before his fingers turned to other places. Her nipples, her bottom, feeling his way around her until she could no longer lie still.

In response she ventured in the same manner across him, stopping as he looked at her.

'Is this allowed?'

'Everything is. There is nothing forbidden in any of it. Only choice.'

She licked his throat and tasted salt, and then she sucked his skin in the way he had hers, leaving a red whorl, marking him as hers. The joy in it was exhilarating. She could play with his body without censure? Her hands crept lower and she stroked him, his sex moving with each ministration and hardening further. Power consumed her. Making love was something done together, with consent, with gladness, with the building passion guiding her, letting her know the way.

She wanted him in her, holding him there, and she moved against him as he came across her and opened her legs.

A finger slipped inside, and then another and then his member was pushing up and up until the largeness filled her and she felt him in all the places no one had ever touched before, every nerve inside glowing and reaching and wanting.

Her release came on his final push as they strained together, rigid with passion and never wanting an end.

Paradise.

She had been transported there, the wetness between them attesting to the beauty of it, even as she kept him within.

Lust had a language that was undeniable and wonderful. She could feel neither guilt nor shame nor worry.

Much later she woke in another room on a wide bed with a velvet cover pulled across her and the moonlight slanting in.

He was sitting beside her, watching. He still wore his white shirt, wrinkled now from their exertions, and there was a smile on his face. He looked so much younger like this; gone was the stern aristocrat and in his place was the quieter version of a contented lover.

'How did we get here?' She rubbed her eyes and looked around. 'And where is here?'

'You are in my bedroom and I carried you up.'

Her petticoat had been removed and her hair fell all around her face, the pins gone. The memories of the evening rushed in and she felt the blush on her cheeks rising. They had made love three times after the first at various hours of the night and in different ways. He was not a prig in the art of sex and she was very glad of it. She felt sated and sensual and satisfied.

'Delight was everything I had hoped for.' She stated this quietly because truth seemed important between them.

The smile on his face broadened. 'I could say exactly the same.'

Bringing her in against him, she felt his fingers tracing shapes softly across her skin and in the darkness honesty seemed important.

'My husband was always angry with me, especially after he realised I could not conceive a child.'

His fingers stopped their tracing and rested on her. 'In all honesty I am probably the same, as Gretel and I tried hard enough to conceive at first. This way there are no complications in our delight, no extra worries. A simple, easy and sensual life. What could be better?'

She began to laugh and the moment between them that could have been terrible was beautiful instead.

'You do not have a hankering for heirs?' She asked this gently.

'I don't because I already have them in Oliver's

sons. Two estates, two boys and more than enough money to see that Juliette is well provided for as well.'

He sounded as if he genuinely meant it and the emptiness that had always been inside her as a result of her inability to bear a child was filled instead with something else entirely. Acceptance perhaps and relief. When his fingers began to move again she shut her eyes and enjoyed the feeling until the clock in the corner rang out the hour of four and she knew she should leave before too much longer.

But he turned her into him and this time he was neither gentle nor temperate. No, this time he kissed her in a way that had her accepting everything he was seeking and more.

He had seen her off into his carriage, her clothes, hat and coat all again in place and her hair retied into a knot at the nape. The hour of five was already upon them and to be seen in the daylight hours alone in a coach after an entire night out would be ruinous for any woman.

He could not accompany her, either, for the very same reason.

A hidden affair. An illicit coupling. A sensual escapade that he could barely believe had just happened. He was almost thirty-three and he had never once in all his life felt like this. Breathless. Yearning for more. Wanting it with an ache.

They were now in a place that set them aside from the normal world, a place of veiled secrecy and clandestine emotion. There was an excitement to it as well as a thrilling fear of being caught.

He looked at his left hand and saw the paleness of his skin where his ring had sat for so many years. He had taken it off a week ago because it did not feel right to wear it, given the thoughts he was having about Wilhelmina. Gretel's sickness was a part of the equation too, the guilt of her passing still in him, the idea that he may not have done enough for her in her life, may not have loved her as he should have even though he had tried his very hardest.

He had placed his ring in her glory box, the one sent with her to Elmsworth on her marriage to him, full of things that had never been taken out, baby clothes, a small knitted blanket and toys that she had held dear as a child: a felt bunny, a leather ball stitched together in red wool, a rattle for teething with both a pink and a blue ribbon tied around the handle.

Dreams and hopes in their tangible form. Aspirations that had never come to pass.

Perhaps it was all these things that had made him think he was not a man meant to be a husband, that his one foray into marriage had been so loss-filled he never wanted another one.

He looked out into the early morning light, a pink sky rising in the east. He missed Wilhelmina already, missed who he became with her, missed the sensual heat of sex. For the first time in a long while his hands felt warm and they did not shake. He wondered what would happen next between them and he also feared what might not.

Willa could not find sleep even though she had had very little in all of her long and wondrous night with Phillip Moreland.

She felt different, that was the trouble. She felt fulfilled. Her fingers went down to the place between her legs, feeling the wetness as a gift. She had not bathed. She wanted to keep the scent of him with her for as long as she was able. She wanted him in her again, filling her, heating her, making her whole. Her hips moved up and down in rhythm as she pleasured herself, quietly and with intent. The Earl had released something in her that could not be stoppered, a primal hunger that could be fed only by him.

When would they meet again and where? Today? Tonight? She would like to make love in the sunshine outside in green fields or in his carriage on the way to a public ball where he might lift her skirts and come into her. Unseen by others. Known only to them.

Her release came quickly with these thoughts and she held herself still as her body throbbed into ecstasy. And then she slept.

The next night she dismissed all her staff early. He came to her just as the darkness turned and she led him to her room without speaking. She wore only a cream satin slip, which he removed within a few seconds and then they were on her bed, desperate for the taste of each other.

It was different this time. Fervent and reckless, as if the hours they had been apart all had to be accounted for in pounds of flesh and in heartbeats, and when he sank into her finally he groaned in a way she had not heard the night before. Like a wounded animal. Like a man who was uncertain of his fate.

'You are like a drug, Wilhelmina. A drug I cannot stop wanting.'

And she felt the same way about him. Theirs was not the quiet gentleness of a pairing with all the time in the world. No, they tore at each other without boundaries, with a carnal need that could only be assuaged by the body of the other. Only when she felt him deep inside her was she complete, holding him there until release throbbed between them and they were still.

She did not wish for words tonight, and when he tried to speak again she placed her fingers across his lips and stopped him.

'Just now. Just us.' And he was quiet, the dark blue in his eyes brushed with lust.

This was how she wanted it. Knowing each other without a past or a future, finding delight in every touch and every kiss. Understanding that the pain of making love held a message too, in the slick wetness of their coupling. He was not always gentle and she was not always kind, and when he left three hours later she watched him from her window and wondered exactly who she had become.

A different woman. A freer one. A brazen mistress who relished everything that he showed her and was ashamed of nothing.

One hand cradled her stomach as if inside things were changing, as if the dry and barren woman she had always been had a new beginning, and all she could feel was hope.

Phillip sat in his carriage and swore.

He wanted her again the minute he had left her, the surge of sex so very welcome after years of nothing.

Perhaps that was why he felt like this? Never satisfied. Restless. Desperate. To have her again and to understand in the act of plunder there was also an undercurrent of a need so great he could not bear it.

Everything he had believed to be true in his life was suddenly shattered into pieces. Marriage. Love. Distance. False hope.

He had protected Gretel from the first moment of meeting her and had lost himself in doing so. He had believed in the prophesies of his mad and damaged mother, a woman who eschewed closeness and honesty. He had listened to the advice of his father, who refused to believe one could not change or reform an unsuitable wife.

He had thought celibacy was the answer for a prayer of redemption and the hope of Gretel's healing.

He had failed himself in the dread of it all.

Until now.

Willa had touched something in him that made him live and hope. and Gretel's sadness and distance floated further away, into a place where he could remember her without despair. A small miracle, he thought as he conjured up Willa's golden eyes and sensual body. A woman of strength and honesty and the sort of beauty that drove a man mad.

Chapter Ten

The next afternoon Wilhelmina met with Anna Cherton in town. Given the lateness of her assignation with Phillip Moreland last night she wished the arrangements had not been made a week or so before. If she did not come, though, Anna would wonder why and so, even though it was the last thing she wished to be doing, she found herself in the window seat of Gunter's in Regent Street just before half-past two.

Willa had loved this place since arriving in London, for the tantalising treats of pastries, sweets and ice cream never disappointed; it was just today she was tired and wanted to be by herself to relive the night she had just spent with Phillip.

As they were escorted to their seats her glance scanned across the many other patrons in the room; family groups and friends all enjoying the atmosphere. Gunter's was like a small wonderland after the strict parsimoniousness at Belton Park, the range of delicacies still astonishing to Willa, even after her years of being in town.

'Isn't it just magical?' Anna, by her side, had a wide smile on her face as she rearranged her skirts to a good advantage. 'It never becomes monotonous, either, because they change things so much and it is always delicious. I think because it is such a warm afternoon I am going to have ice cream in the orange and lemon flavourings to keep cool. After that I shall choose a pastry and perhaps a small bowl of my favourite sweets.'

Today they were both wearing pink, Willa's gown a darker shade than Anna's. She seldom wore this colour but the warm blue summer morning had made her choose it from her wardrobe. Perhaps the shade was a bit girlish for her but today she could not care because she felt so happy, the delight from last night still very much inside her.

'You did not come to the Taylors' soiree yesterday or the Smithsons' luncheon, Willa. I looked for you especially.'

Wilhelmina found lying hard and a blush of discomfort made her face hot.

'I've been busy.' Not a fib but not quite the truth either.

'Did you know that George Fitzgibbon has left for the Continent already?'

She nodded. 'I had heard he was going.'

'He blames you for his needing to leave London.'

This surprised her even as Anna continued speaking.

'He told me you had refused his offer of marriage and he had no more wish to remain in your circle, given such a rebuff. I think actually, Wilhelmina, he was genuinely hurt when you suggested he pursue Miss Leonora Blanchard instead as a suitable bride. You were not so interchangeable to him.'

'Which I am sorry for but can do nothing about. Everyone in London knows that I will never marry again after my first disastrous union, and who would blame me? I told George this myself a year or more ago and if he fails to accept it as truth, what else can I do?'

'You danced with Phillip Moreland twice at the Kellands' ball. Sharon Picton and Amelia Drummond told me you looked quite the pair.'

'Then I think they might both need spectacles so that they can see properly.' To change the subject Willa called the waiter over and in consultation with Anna they made two orders of ice cream to begin with.

And it was then she noticed him through the window, dressed in black and crossing the road towards them on the street outside.

Every time she saw Phillip Moreland anew Willa was astonished by his beauty but here in public today it was completely different. She knew that beauty intimately now and the same want she had experienced yesterday began to creep inside unbidden as he walked through the front door into the tea shop.

'Lord Elmsworth.' Willa tried for a nonchalance she was far from feeling.

'Mrs St Claire.' His effort was far better than hers. 'Miss Cherton.'

The perfect gentleman. The perfect lover. Willa had always known that he had kept his secrets hidden, so why was she not surprised here? But there was a disappointment, too, because when she met his eyes he looked into hers without passion. And it hurt.

'Would you join us for an ice, my lord, on this warm afternoon?' Anna's voice was flirtatious and that fact gave Willa a hollow and awful feeling.

'I am afraid that I cannot, Miss Cherton, for I have a meeting I need to be at in a few minutes.'

'Well, I wish to tell you that you have been missed at the recent events in Society, Lord Elmsworth, for everyone has been asking after you.'

'I have been busy.'

He was speaking about their lovemaking, Willa

knew that he was, and a warm feeling spread across her, although when she looked up she saw Anna watching her and clamped down on her thoughts in consternation.

'Willa has just told me exactly the same and it is such a bother, for these soirees are starting to feel very empty. Would you not agree, Willa?'

'Perhaps,' she began and then stopped. With the Earl looking at her directly now she could barely remember Anna's question. The blue in his eyes was darker here, the silver almost disappeared. Different eyes than the ones that had taken in all of her nakedness late last night.

But he had moved back now, and as he replaced his hat he bade them both good day and left, walking across the road towards Bond Street with that particular and easy gait of his.

'I hope you know what you are doing, Wilhelmina.'

Anna seldom called her by her full name, so Willa knew exactly what was coming.

'The Earl of Elmsworth will need a wife and heirs. It is the way of these ancient aristocratic families and you will only be hurt by the scandal should you imagine it otherwise.'

'Phillip Moreland is a friend.' She tried to imbue that statement with nonchalance and sternness.

'Oh, please, Willa. If I am noticing the spark between you both, others soon will be, too. You have a place here in London that is solidified by your reputation of widowhood and wisdom. Silly women with air in their heads might make the same mistake, but you…'

'I am fine.'

'I don't think you are.' Anna's voice was lower still now, worry easily discernible. 'I don't want to see you crucified by Society's unwritten protocols. You are not from a family of the first water, Wilhelmina, and even though you have risen up the ranks of the social ladder by intelligence and talent it will not take much for those who are jealous of you to plot and throw you off. And believe me they will, because that is how it works here and every one of those jealous mamas and their daughters will want the Earl of Elmsworth for themselves. I am your friend, Wilhelmina, and I am warning you. Do not continue this affair, for it will lead to ruination.'

Willa took in a breath and gathered her courage. 'I know you mean well, Anna, and I appreciate it, but you are worrying about something that does not exist.'

But her friend was not one to give up so easily. 'Why don't we take a trip to the Continent, you and I? We could wind our way through the sights of

France and head to Italy. I have a second cousin in Paris who would love to show us his city and it would be a good break for us both.'

Willa put one hand over Anna's. 'You have always been a friend and I know what you are doing, but I do not need protecting.'

'Very well, I will say no more, but if you ever wish to talk I am here.'

'And I thank you for it.'

Much, much later she and Phillip lay in each other's arms and watched the stars in the night sky through the opened windows of his bedroom, the endless blackness dotted with lights.

'If you could make one wish here and now, what would it be?' she said softly, noting the cluster of Pleiades bright in the northwest.

'I'd wish that everything would disappear and we could be alone together in the country at Elmsworth Manor.'

A smile surfaced.

'It might be more difficult to be so discreet there, and social acceptance in the countryside can be very traditional, particularly on an estate such as yours.'

He did not answer, and his silence was somehow jarring. Did he agree? Was he already tiring of her?

Is this what happened in the sensual world of the Bon Ton? A quick affair and then an end?

To take her mind off such a problem she stroked the fourth finger of his left hand. 'What happened to your wedding ring?'

'I took it off because it felt wrong to keep on wearing it, here like this.'

'Because of Gretel and her promise of abstinence? The one that she wanted you to adhere to forever?'

He frowned. 'No, because it felt like a symbol which made moving on difficult.'

'And you have now? Moved on?'

'How can you ask me that after the past few nights?'

In his question, the disquiet pressing close shifted further away. They were not hurting anyone. They were just living.

'Stay with me till the morning, Willa. Don't go home.'

'I think you should know that Anna asked me today at Gunter's whether we were lovers. She said she'd noticed a spark between us and if she could see it she said that others would too. She urged care.'

'We are older. We have both been married. We are immune from all the silly rules Society sets out so arbitrarily.'

'You may be, my Lord Elmsworth,' she drawled,

'but I am not, for a double standard applies only to the upper echelons. My background is more lowly and I could easily be placed beyond the social pale with my behaviour should we be discovered.'

He rolled her over and lay on top, looking down at her with a wicked smile on his face. 'I will protect you, I promise.'

'How?' Two could play at this game.

'By whisking you away to the very ends of the land and having my way with you. Like this.' His mouth covered one nipple and he played with the hardening bud against his tongue. 'And like this.' Further down he went, the cold trail of his mouth making her shiver with delight. 'And then like this.' He opened her legs and found her centre, his forefinger on the place where all feelings came from as she squirmed, wanting more. Which he gave her, with his fingers at first and then with his mouth and then with the hardness of his sex filling her, riding her, on and on as the wispy gauze curtains blew in the breeze and the stars inside her exploded into light and life and loveliness, taking away all the darkness.

He was hers and she was his and there was no space between them. No words either to question the wisdom of what they were doing.

In the morning she saw him by the window looking out at the dawn. He always wore his shirt, she thought next, and wondered why he did not disrobe and lie naked as she did. The cotton was wrinkled from their night together and the buttons at the front were undone.

She remembered undoing them one by one as he had watched but when she had tried to slip the fabric further down from his shoulders he had stopped her with a kiss and then with more.

'Good morning.'

He turned to look at her, his hair tousled and the dark shadow of a twelve-hour beard on his face. He looked as if she had caught him out and was slightly surprised, and when she glanced down his manhood was fully aroused and waiting for her.

She smiled and he came to her then, fitting himself around her before driving in, without preamble, without softness, pushing further and further, and keeping her there. Still. Waiting. The drum of blood. A growing answer deep within her and his returning one. With only a little movement he brought her to a place she could barely contemplate, a spiralling hot want that struck her, unbidden, twisting her insides, making her shout out his name, her nails against his back under the shirt clamping him still.

On and on until there was nothing left of sense or place but only feeling, only this. Only them.

And then she slept.

When she woke he was fully dressed and sitting on a chair by the bed, watching her. In his hands he held a small framed drawing which he passed to her.

The woman in it was the most beautiful female Willa had ever seen, with her blue eyes, blonde hair, pointed chin and her head at a slight angle as if the world amused her but she did not know why. Willa knew who she was immediately because she had briefly glimpsed her once and heard all the many and varied descriptions of the incomparable Miss Gretel Carmichael.

'I wanted you to see what my wife looked like.'

She sat up, pulling the sheets around her. The Golden Girl. The debutante who had set the Ton alight with her beauty.

'When was this done?'

'Two years after we married. It was her Christmas present to me.'

'No wonder you miss her. All that beauty and promise…'

'You asked me once if I had tried to kill my brother and I said I had meant to miss. The reason for it all was Gretel.' He took in a breath. 'She was sick, much more sick than any of us realised, and she was desperate to conceive a child. I told you we had tried but had had no luck, and perhaps she thought it was my fault, which it may well have been. But she went to see my brother and asked him to give her the baby that I could not, the heir to Elmsworth. I swear that I knew none of this until she confessed what she had done a month or so before her death.'

Willa saw in Phillip the sadness that was so much of who he was, the aching chasm of guilt that showed in his eyes and on his face as he told the story.

'Oliver refused, of course, and Gretel retaliated by telling me that he had then tried to take advantage of her. There was a bruise on her arm and her hand was cut, so I had no reason to believe that he had not, such was her power over most men. I went to see my brother to give him a stern warning never to come near us again and to protect the name of our forebears, but as I pointed the pistol away my hand started shaking and it went off…' He frowned. 'My mother's hands shook the same way mine do and perhaps I have inherited the condition, though of late with you here I have not noticed it so much.'

Willa got out of bed and stood beside him. 'You did not kill him, Phillip. Oliver is alive.'

'By luck only. And after that Gretel deteriorated markedly, for I could see the difference in her day by day.'

'She was sick. That was not your fault, either.'

'I think I harm people, Wilhelmina. Everyone who comes close to me gets hurt and I want you to be safe. I should never have had that gun in my hand and I still cannot be sure why I did. I have not touched a firearm since.'

Willa took in a breath, understanding what this was about. The Arrogant Earl had been his nickname here in Society before he had gone to America. The Distant Earl was another name she had heard and they both made sense. It was protection he was trying to offer, protection from himself.

'Everyone has their skeletons and secrets. I know that I have mine. I told you once that Lionel had died by falling off the balcony onto the paving below. But what I did not say is that I had pushed him to stop him ripping out the pages of my diary, which he had grabbed. He went over the edge shouting to the world around him that it was my fault. And it was in a way, in the same way of you shooting your brother. Not by design but by chance.'

When he did not reply she kept going. Better for him to know the truth than to learn a lesser version of it from someone else.

'Lionel's shoe caught on the jutting edge of the stones and that was all it took. And when he fell I rushed to the edge and looked down and I did not feel guilty or sad. I felt relief. I felt freedom. I felt the weight of all my life lifted off my shoulders even as the servants came rushing to help and his blood was spreading dark beneath him on the grey of the pavers.'

She began to shake with the coldness of the room on her naked body and he lifted a blanket from the bed and tucked it around her, bringing her into him.

'I think it wasn't your fault.' His words were whispered into her hair.

'And I think that it was not yours, either.'

Sanctuary coupled with absolution was a potent thing as she wrapped herself further around him and held on until her tears stopped and there was nothing left save for relief.

'We were both married to people who could never be happy and suffered because of it.' He held her tight before speaking again. 'But here with you in my arms, all I can think of is how right it is and how I never want it to end.'

For the next few weeks they met every night, either at her place or his, quietly and in secret, two people who needed the other to make them whole, clinging to delight with every fibre of themselves.

Willa could not remember a time when she had been so happy, and the nights turned into daylight assignations as well. Phillip had sent most of his staff to Elmsworth Manor in Hampshire to help out there for a month, so the town house on St James Square was theirs, except for an elderly cook and her husband whose living quarters were off the kitchen, and whom they seldom saw.

It was a perfect arrangement.

This afternoon they lay on a bed in the bedroom upstairs in the front of the house, the sun from the large windows slanting in across them.

'In America I thought I might never be happy again. I could never have imagined this.' Phillip's finger trailed up the curve of one breast and then to her throat. 'You have the softest skin, Willa, and in the sun here it glows golden.'

She laughed.

'My mother had the same skin because her ancestors hailed from northern France.'

'Did you have other family with you in Hampshire when you were growing up?'

'No, there was none. Both my parents were only children whose parents had died a long time before I was born. I think that was why they clung to each other so desperately and why they could never understand what my needs as a child were. You were lucky to have a brother.'

'I didn't feel that way for a long time but now, with Esther and the children, we are growing closer and it feels right.'

'This feels right, too,' she returned as his fingers

trailed down her stomach and rested in the space between her legs.

And then they spoke to each other in different ways, the body having a language all of its own.

Chapter Eleven

Lionel's cousin Simon St Claire came to visit Willa the next afternoon in Russell Square. He was a large man whom she had never liked and today he looked angrier than she had ever seen him. After barely giving her a greeting he got straight to the point.

'I have had word from my lawyer to say that the sale of Belton Park is going ahead. I warned you not to try to sell it until I had all the family papers in order and I am here today to repeat my warning. Lionel did not wish for his house and land to go to you. He wanted it to go to a continuation of the St Claire line after you supplied my cousin with neither progeny nor happiness.'

His face was puffy and red and he wiped his forehead with a handkerchief pulled from his pocket. 'I will fight this sale until the last breath I take and I won't be kind.'

'Are you threatening me, Mr St Claire?'

'I am, madam. I am threatening you because you are a whore and a murderer. It is said that you pushed my cousin from the balcony with intent and then you slept with the lawyer who came to the Park a few days later to give you the details of your dead husband's will.'

Dread filled her. This was everything she had always feared, laid out with such vitriol and threat. She could disprove none of it either, for she was certain Simon St Claire would have gathered credible witnesses to add to his accusations.

Shame washed in, a huge wave of it, for her stupidity, for Lionel's lack of care and for Mr Elliott MacDonald, who had taken her hand in his with care and tried to explain the workings of the law. The first soft touch she had had in years. Another mistake on top of all the ones she had made. She waited to see what Lionel's cousin would say next.

'We can do this in two ways. I can bring forth all my evidence to a judge in a court of law or you can simply walk away with five thousand pounds and the chance to start anew somewhere else, far from London, somewhere away from any reminders of your former life, somewhere so distant that we should never have to see each other again.'

He took out a sheet of paper then and laid it down before her. It outlined the transgressions of Mr Elliott

MacDonald and Wilhelmina's inappropriate behaviour with him in the days following the death of her husband. She wondered where Simon St Claire could have got such private information but everything on the sheet was true, so she stayed silent. This was a form of blackmail, a threat to expose her behaviour to the world should she not do as he wanted.

He then showed her another letter. This one was crudely signed at the bottom by one of the gardeners employed at Belton Park.

'This man, Mr Trevor Dell, says that he saw you shove my cousin away from you. He was in the garden at the time and, hearing shouts, he looked up. He said Lionel's last words were, "Your fault" as he fell. He presumed it to mean that his wife, Mrs Wilhelmina St Claire, had pushed him to his death.'

Then he took out a further list and laid it down in front of her. On it were the times the carriage of the Earl of Elmsworth had visited her town house across the past week as well as the times she had visited his town house.

He had been watching her house and her movements from some vantage point, or perhaps he had had others do it for him. But he was not yet finished with his insults.

'You take men and twist them into puppets to do exactly as you will, with no mind at all for decency or morality. Well, your schemes are finished, madam, and I will shout out your debauchery and evil from every rooftop in London if you do not sign the rights of Belton Park back to my family, an act that ought to have happened when my cousin died.'

When she looked down she saw the ownership deed, even as he laid a pen and an ink pot down for her to sign it with.

'Our family land was never supposed to be yours. It should have always been protected, given you could not provide suitable heirs to ensure its safety.' His voice was rough and full of impatience.

Willa thought of Phillip Moreland and what he would think of her. She thought of those moments with him that had been like Heaven. She thought of his hurt and of the ways this would hurt him further. She thought of how she would be cut from London Society forever if even just a whiff of all this got out.

'If I sign this I would need proof that this would be the end of your blackmail. Lionel's falling was an accident only. He was an abusive man, so when Elliott MacDonald offered some kindness to me after my husband's death I took it.'

She said nothing of Phillip Moreland. That was all she could do to protect him. She knew ruin was like dropping a pebble in the middle of a still pond and that the rings of wreckage would get bigger and bigger. She could not drag the Earl of Elmsworth into the melee of the disaster that she had created. But she could not trust Simon St Claire either as she needed time to get her affairs into order.

'I need a month to vacate my rented town house and leave. Come back to me after that time and I will sign the transfer of Belton Park into your hands and leave London for good. But I will only do that if you keep these accusations to yourself and I am left alone. I do not wish for further threats of exposure and if you do not agree to such terms then you risk years of this matter dragging through the legal channels, and believe me I will fight the charges.'

He looked so angry Willa thought he might hit her, but she stood her ground and said nothing else and finally he nodded, collected his papers and left.

The horror of everything began to hit her. If she could not disprove these claims, could she be hung for the murder of her husband? Or be banished to prison for years?

She had to keep the allegations out of the public domain in any way she could and Simon St Claire's greed was the only route that was possible.

One month. One month to leave her old life and to try to shield Phillip from the awfulness of her past.

* * *

Phillip came to her later that evening, as he had meetings in the city with his lawyers.

She was in the little blue salon just off the front entrance when she heard his voice and, standing up, she waited for him to reach for her, all his safety and strength gathering her in.

Protection.

It was a feeling she had never known before and she closed her eyes and leant against him, relief rising from the worry.

'You are back.' She tipped her head to accept his kiss. 'Are you hungry?'

'Just for you.'

It felt so good to laugh even amidst all the danger of what would come. Untying her nightgown, she let it fall to the floor. Underneath she wore nothing but her skin.

This time she made the first move, running her hand across his cheek and then pulling at the tails of his neck cloth. He went to help her but she stopped him.

'It's my turn.'

When the tie was gone she undid the buttons of his shirt, one by one.

'Can I take it off?'

He looked almost uncertain before he nodded, and

she pushed the sleeves across his arms and it fell to the floor. Three strips of scarred flesh wrapped across the top of his arm and then curled down his back. This was what he had tried to hide on all the other nights, though she had felt the ridges in the darkness.

'They are knife wounds.'

'Why?'

'God knows, because I certainly do not.'

When he said no more she leant forward and kissed the scars, running her tongue gently across the hurt. He stayed silent, though she felt a heavy tremor run through him.

'Sometimes life is unfair.' Her words were soft as her hands went to his belt and the flap of his trousers. With only a small effort both fell away and he bent to unbuckle his boots.

Then he was as naked as she was, the lamp on the sideboard slanting across him, his muscles catching light and shadow in startling definition. Not an indolent lord but a man who had used his body in all of the right ways. Tears came to her eyes at the thought of the lonely miles he must have endured in America after the death of his wife.

With all the care in the world she took his nipple between her thumb and forefinger, slowly rubbing at first and then when she increased the speed their eyes locked on to each other's. She saw shock there and then delight, she saw the smouldering flame quicken and burst, his breathing deeper, his other nipple hardening in unison.

'Take me.' His words now.

And so she did. She made him lie down on the rug and she sat astride him, guiding him into her and rolling her body, the slick, wet sound of their joining urging them on. Two halves making a whole. It was all she could give him now. Beauty and memory and truth. It was no longer just carnal and fleeting, the eroticism changed to something so much more.

Us, she said without words and with a tenderness that had been missing before, a soul touching honesty that could not be misinterpreted.

I love you.

For a moment she thought she might have said it out loud but she had not. It was her insides welling with a knowledge of all she would miss out on and all she would lose. She could not tell him because it would be his ruination and she had enough sense still to know it.

And when they both rose to the heights of ecstasy she let every part of herself go in a way she had not before and felt his seed fill her with the pleasure of release as she gripped him with her thighs, her breath taken, her thoughts scattered into just this moment, *now.*

* * *

In the very early hours of the morning they woke and went to the kitchen to find something to eat because they were hungry.

'This reminds me of the first time we met,' he said as she laid out some bread and cheese on a platter before him.

'I was overwhelmed by you, I remember. I talked too much.'

'I never minded that.' He smiled as he said it. 'I liked the way you surprised me. I still do. Oliver sent word today that he and Esther will be in London next week. They are staying with the Duggans but would like to see us.'

'I am glad for it.'

He frowned at her tone and took her hand. 'You sound sad.'

'I just know how quickly life can change from one thing to another, and family is important.'

'Do you miss yours?'

'No, because we were not a close group, but I sense with Oliver and you that it was different.'

'I know I will never have offspring to inherit Elmsworth and so it is important for me to understand their children.'

Wilhelmina took his hand and kissed the back of it. It was on the tip of her tongue to tell him he should have heirs and a wife and a chance at the life she could never give him, in Society amongst all that he knew as the Earl of Elmsworth. But she could not get the words out and was too selfish to even try.

Not now, not after their lovemaking, not in the darkness of night after such perfection. For this moment she could still pretend it was just them against the world and no one was crouching in the shadows, getting ready to ruin everything.

For this moment she liked the feel of him on her body, the wetness between her legs, the swelling fullness of her lips, the pink whorls on her breasts where he had sucked her as she had gone to sleep.

She was a woman who had known the very pinnacle of everything that was sensual, the pain and the pleasure, the soft and the hard.

So when he led her up the stairs after their late-night snack and laid her down on her bed she could only welcome him in, another time, a further wonder, an inexplicable and miraculous union that she had no words to even try to describe.

She shut her eyes instead and let herself simply feel.

Him. Them. Love.

Chapter Twelve

The following morning Wilhelmina sat down to write to Phillip explaining that she had business out of London and would be back in a week. She knew he would have questions and that he would not be pleased but she couldn't risk a continuation of their relationship in its current form.

The problem was that her feelings were now involved and the delight she had sought at first had begun to be something else entirely.

She loved him. She did. She loved Phillip Moreland with all her heart and soul.

This realisation took her breath away as much as it frightened her. She could never tell him and she could not expect the same back. He had been honest with her from the start that this was a physical relationship only, because he still mourned his deceased wife, and that he would not marry again. He had never once, even in the heat of passion, whispered permanent words or promised more.

And now, with Simon St Claire threatening to expose her, she understood she would need to leave Phillip to the life he was meant for: in the best circles of Society as the head of the Elmsworth title so that he could find his place here and flourish.

She would travel down to Royal Tunbridge Wells this very day to see the McAllistair sisters and arrange accommodation for herself within the area. Being so out of touch would allow for things to settle between the Earl and her, and when she saw him again she hoped she could make him understand that their chosen path as lovers had not been a wise one.

Phillip spent the following morning with his estate manager going over the plans for the next few months on the estate. He enjoyed these meetings because it allowed him to be so much more involved in the future of the land that had been in his family for centuries.

This part of his return to England had been a revelation to him as before he had left he had not felt the same sort of connection. Now he could see that his part in the tapestry of Elmsworth's history was important and it had been one of the joys of his coming home.

But by the early afternoon he wanted to be back with Wilhelmina, making love, forgetting everything, living in a world where nothing mattered save for the pleasures of the flesh.

He'd never been a man who had been devoured by lust but here he was, his body aching and fidgety for the power of sex. A different man from the husband he had been with Gretel, where touching and making love was so much more mundane and deliberate and where weeks or months could go by before any urges surfaced on both their parts.

Gretel had never let go of her inhibitions as Wilhelmina did. She had never explored the darker side of sex, where anything was sanctioned so long as it was consensual. He had never spent as many hours in bed as happily as he had with Willa either, hungry for each other, never quite sated.

This realisation made him stand still.

He had imagined himself as a contained person, little stirring his emotions in the way others seemed to be stirred, and yet now…

His world had exploded into colour and feeling, all the base and raw instincts so much more accessible and taking over from the man he had been.

He held out his right hand into a horizontal position and observed it. His fingers had stopped shaking. The carnal realm had been good for him, for it stopped him thinking so much about his past and his future, and the anxiety he had always been bothered by had lessened.

The note from Willa came just as he was tidying all his papers and readying himself to make his way to her house.

Her words informed him that she had gone south for seven days or so on business and yet she had told him nothing at all of it last night.

He knew so little about her life here or even about the one before outside of Winchester, and he had told her as few facts about his past. Existing in the present as they had been had its advantages but it also had its drawbacks.

Seven days. It seemed like an inordinate amount of time, feeling, as he did, desperate for her body. Was this how other men felt, was his next thought, those men who sought out mistresses and courtesans and who prior to this he had had no understanding of at all?

He only wanted Willa. That was also the trouble. He liked the way she smelt and the way her mind worked. He liked her sensuality and her smile.

Seven days.

He would return to Hampshire until she was back, for without her by his side London seemed pointless. He would visit his brother and go riding across the

Elmsworth land. He would see his tenants too, one by one, and find out their needs, which was a thing long overdue, and all these activities would help to pass the time.

A colder thought slid into these. Perhaps Wilhelmina did not feel the same way he did and wanted some distance. Perhaps this was how these blazing affairs of the heart ran their course, burning bright and then quickly dying.

He wanted more. He wanted her with him forever in any form that would suit her. A long-term mistress? A wife? That thought had him leaning forward.

He closed his eyes and stood there, his world bent so suddenly out of shape it was disconcerting. If he asked her to marry him what would she say? They had always been so dismissive of the idea but now… now it was all he could think of, a union that was legally ordained and permanent. Would she think the same? For him this affair of the flesh had become so much more and he missed her every hour that they were apart.

His glance fell to the ring-less third finger on his left hand and he touched the skin there. Gretel's demands and melancholy no longer affected him as they had used to and he wanted to move on from the regret of his first marriage. He wanted to live again and laugh. With Wilhelmina.

After sending her note to Phillip, Willa had travelled to Tunbridge Wells with only a small suitcase and rented a room not far from the McAllistair sisters. She needed time to think and plan what was next and had arranged for all the possessions from her apartment to be boxed up and held in storage until she decided what she would do permanently.

Simon St Claire had arrived in Royal Tunbridge Wells on the fifth day she'd been there, unannounced and spiteful, his words full of retribution.

'I think it only reasonable, given our dealings over Belton Park, that you let me know where you are so I can contact you.'

'How did you find me?'

'I thought that you might leave and so I had your town house watched. It was easy to track you.'

Horror flooded through her. She should never have trusted him to allow her the month.

'But I am here to tell you today that I am tired of this cat and mouse game.' He laid the deeds of Belton Park on the table before her. 'Now sign the damn thing for I have run out of patience. You have had two years of income from the wealth of the land as well as all the money my cousin saved up across the years. His bank account was empty when I looked into it.'

'I think you might understand why,' she gave back, anger now rising. 'I was your cousin's legal wife for over ten long years.'

'You were a miserable wife with your lack of progeny and constant sadness, and Lionel was tired of you after the very first year. He told me so again and again. Now sign it. I will have Mr MacDonald bring you back a copy.'

'No. I do not wish to see him.'

He smiled. 'The evils of the past have a way of coming back, Mrs St Claire, and a loose woman like you would probably enjoy an extra bit of male companionship when it is offered.'

Fear flared inside her at the leer Lionel's cousin gave her as he reached out to run a finger along her cheekbone. 'You are a widow and alone. Would any man at all do?'

'Get out.'

He laughed.

'You are almost beautiful when you are angry. Did you know that? And no one at all would come to help you if you screamed. Lionel was a fool not to enjoy you more but he always had his head in the stars, whereas I…' He stopped. 'I have always appreciated a shapely woman.' His hand cupped her breast and squeezed hard, the shock of it making her shake.

'The only way I will sign this paper is if you wait outside.'

He looked uncertain for a moment.

'I shall give you to the count of three. One... two...'

He was gone before she reached three and she picked up his pen and signed the document, knowing that if she did not everything would be far more dangerous. She had done this to herself by leaving London. She had not thought out this plan at all and now was paying the price for her stupidity.

If Simon came back she knew he would assault her, for she could see his evil intention in his eyes, and so without thinking more she ran through the back door, along the row of trees that sheltered her from the front of the house, and down the lane across the fields.

Once in the small village she relaxed a bit and walked more slowly towards the cottage of the McAllistair sisters. She could not stay and involve them further but she would say a quick goodbye. Everything was perilous and nowhere was safe.

She knew Simon St Claire would not keep to his word either. Her name would be bandied around before long and tagged with all the horrible things he had accused her of. There was only a small amount of time for her to disappear entirely but before she did she had one last thing to do.

Willa knocked at the door of Phillip Moreland's town house just before the hour of three the next afternoon. Her heart was beating like a drum in her chest and she felt clammy but she made herself stand still and take in a breath.

The butler took her directly through to the library and then the Earl was in front of her, beautiful and smiling. He was dressed today in dark blue.

Rising from the seat behind his desk, he walked towards her. 'I wondered which day you would return, Willa, and I must say that I am very glad to see you back.'

Her heart broke again as she swallowed, waiting until his servant closed the door behind him. Phillip had stopped now just out of reach, a frown upon his brow, as if he could tell she was upset about something.

'While I was gone I have been thinking…about our relationship.'

The blue in his eyes silvered.

'I have been thinking about all the things that would be impossible to accomplish should we keep on going the way we are. For one I think that you should have your own heirs and to do that you need to be married. It seems the problem of infertility is seldom the man's fault and it may have been Gretel's sickness that stopped her from conceiving. I know that you may say now such a thing does not matter to you but there will come a day when you will wish differently.' She had rehearsed this but the words that spouted out sounded wooden and strange even to her ears.

The Earl stood very still, his face unreadable.

'What has happened since I have been gone, Wilhelmina? Why are you saying these things?'

'Because I don't wish to stop you being happy. I am barren and I do not care to ever be married again. But you…' She took stock and made herself go on. 'Everyone in Society will expect you to take a wife. Our relationship is a more transient one and in a year or in two, when delight fades, what happens then? What happens when being lovers lessens us both?'

'You honestly think all of this?'

She looked him directly in the eye and lied. 'I do. I believe it has been a lovely interlude and a time that I will never forget but I don't want scandal and I need my independence.

'I am thinking of leaving London after the sale of Belton Park has been finalised. I want to travel and see Europe and I want to be free.'

'You sound like Arabella Montague when you talk like that.'

'Perhaps I am more like her than I realised.'

'Perhaps you are.' The words were not complimentary.

'We never wanted permanency, my lord. We both stressed that. No legal binding. Nothing to regret. An affair that would ultimately have an ending, a way of growth for us both before we moved on to other things. More sensible choices.'

'Then why did you make love to me like you did if you were thinking like this a week ago? It did not seem like an ending at all to my mind.'

'Because you are a good lover and I have appreciated our delight. But I think it unwise to continue something that can only eventually hurt us both, and the longer we go on the harder it will be to simply stop. Then we will hate each other. This way we have a chance to remain friends.'

He turned away, his hands fisted at his sides. Angry. She should have expected that.

'You love Elmsworth Manor. You have recovered the damaged relationship between you and your brother. You have a place here in Society and a way to ensure your future. With me it would be harder, I would just be in the way...'

'Stop. This is your decision, Wilhelmina, not mine. Stop telling me what to think.'

'You are right. It is my decision.'

She couldn't say anything else because to qualify this ending with more would leave them both in limbo and in peril. She needed to be strong.

He looked every inch the Earl again now, his face bland and his bearing prickly. He gave the impression of simply wanting her gone. 'You have my address in Hampshire, Mrs St Claire. If you wish to get in contact with a more honest explanation I would appreciate it, because I do not believe this one.'

She felt her teeth clench together as she pasted a smile on her face. And then she left. She simply turned and opened the door and went through it.

The end. Of her. Of him. Of delight.

Her name was all over the city.

Wilhelmina St Claire. Murderer. Whore. Liar. Cheat.

And her continued absence reinforced the rumour.

It was Oliver who gave Phillip this news when he arrived at Elmsworth Manor from Nettleford Park late one afternoon two weeks later.

Phillip had spent much of the time since being back in Hampshire with his brother and he'd told him a little of his relationship with Willa because his hurt was so huge he could not keep it all in and because being close to Oliver was such a relief after years and years apart.

'Mr Simon St Claire, Lionel St Claire's cousin, has presented papers to a court of law with witnesses for his serious allegations against Wilhelmina St Claire. Your name is in the broadsheets, too, Phillip. It seems someone was following your every movement and recorded all the places and times that you met with her. At your house or at hers and always overnight. Scandal has a certain fervour to it.'

Phillip ignored this. 'What do we know of the man?' His voice was furious.

'Nothing much yet but we can easily find out. Do you believe this gossip?' Oliver framed the question with care.

'No. I believe Simon St Claire wants the house and land back in the family and he sees this as the way to do it. Wilhelmina implied the man had been threatening her and obviously this was how. He found an assortment of witnesses who have a vested interest in lying and slammed her with the threat of legal action.'

'Why the hell would she run, then?'

'I hope it was because she was trying to protect me.'

'From rumour and conjecture? Surely she knows you have dealt with that all your life, just as I have.

You've been together for weeks now. My question is, why the hell wouldn't she know that you'd protect her?'

'Because our relationship was complicated.'

'How complicated?'

'There was never meant to be any permanency. It was completely physical and that was all.'

Unexpectedly Oliver began to laugh. 'God's teeth. You don't know the ways of women, brother. No lady would simply bed a man without it meaning more. Ask Esther. Women simply do not work like that.'

'Willa said she didn't want marriage. I told her I didn't, either. All she wanted was delight.'

'Delight?'

'To feel what it was like to have good sex.'

'And did you?'

'Better than good.'

Another burst of laughter had Phillip standing to speak.

'I'll go across to London and try to work out a plan to clear her name. After that I will go and find her.'

'We. We can find her and bring her back. You can't do this by yourself, Phillip, and I am here to help.'

Before they went back to London, Phillip and Oliver journeyed across to Belton Park the following morning.

Belton Hall was bigger than Phillip had expected it to be but every bit as ugly. It was made of a dark pitted stone and was disproportionately high, giving an instant first impression of the facade almost falling over against a moving sky.

When they knocked at the door a woman who introduced herself as Mrs Heron the housekeeper answered. She said that Mr Simon St Claire had not called in to Belton Park for a month or more now and she was not expecting him back.

Her tone implied she did not think much of the man, and so Phillip took his chance to find out more.

'We are here because we are friends of Mrs Wilhelmina St Claire, and she is in trouble.'

Her demeanour changed instantly as she looked around and gestured them in, closing the door straight away behind them and taking them through to a small salon off the main entrance.

'I have heard talk of the Park's ownership being changed. But my guess is that Mr Simon St Claire threatened Mrs St Claire and she gave in, her being a woman on her own and scared. The former master's wife was an angel, and none of the St Claires ever deserved the likes of her, is what I also think. Her husband was a mean man and his cousin is of exactly the same ilk, and now I am hearing stories of

Mrs St Claire being missing and ideas spun around the why of it, too.'

'She has been accused of murder.' Phillip brought the worst charge up first. 'It is said in the legal document that Mr Simon St Claire has presented that his brother was pushed to his death off an upstairs balcony by his wife.'

'Poppycock. Who was it that said that?'

'The gardener, I think.' Oliver spoke now. 'He was the one who signed his name on the accusation.'

'Trevor Dell, then, a man who can neither read nor write. He is here outside so I shall call him in to ask of it. He has not been himself of late and I can now well understand the reason why.'

A moment later a thin old man in rough clothes stood before them all. He had doffed his hat and held it tightly, looking very scared as he did so.

'Mr Dell. These men here are friends of Mrs St Claire's and they are trying to help her. They said you signed a sheet of paper that accused her of pushing her husband to his death.'

Tears began to trickle from his old rheumy eyes and Trevor Dell wiped them away with a dirty sleeve. 'I did not know what I was supposed to do. Mr Simon St Claire said I'd lose my job here if I didn't sign it at the bottom and so I did. I wrote my few letters and he was gone away. Later I heard that

Mrs St Claire were in trouble and it seemed the letter I signed were a big part of it. Mr Kerrick at the village pub read the article out to me about Mrs St Claire that said I saw her push her husband.'

'So you did not see Mrs St Claire push her husband?'

'I did, but not like how the paper says it. He'd grabbed her special book that she writes in and she tried to get it back and over he went. It were a trip more than a push, I would say. An accident that were brought on by his actions more than anything else.'

Phillip nodded and softened his voice. 'If I wrote up a report of what you have just told us, would you sign this new letter? Mrs Heron and my brother will sign the bottom, too, just to put things right. If Simon St Claire is still in a mind of taking away any of your jobs because of this I can promise you all better ones at my estate, Elmsworth, about fifty miles from here.'

The old man's eyes began to fill with tears as he nodded.

In the afternoon Philip and Oliver found Mr MacDonald in the legal firm of Fox and Pringle halfway down the main street of Winchester. He was a handsome, youngish man who looked nothing like Philip had expected him to.

When he heard why they were there he blushed roundly and showed them into his small office.

'I think I know why you are here. It is because of Wilhelmina, is it not?'

The familiarity of his address irritated Phillip.

'It is, indeed. You have held her up to the world as a loose woman and one for whom you had no respect at all.'

'I loved her,' he blurted out. 'I still love her, but Simon St Claire had all the facts about our short relationship and he wanted to ruin her. It's why I left his legal employ…he has no morals at all.'

'You are the third person today who has told us he is a cheat and a liar. I suggest you draft another letter while we wait, stating Wilhelmina St Claire is nothing like the loose woman Simon St Claire insists she is. The fact is he wanted possession of Belton Park and he did everything in his power to have it.'

An hour later, armed with the two letters, Oliver, Phillip and Esther rode south in the Elmsworth carriage to London, leaving the children at Nettleford Park whilst they dealt with the matter at hand.

Esther could not believe that this had happened to Wilhelmina. 'She is such a generous and good person. But where exactly did you say she is now?'

'We don't know,' Oliver replied. 'In the south, is Phillip's first guess, but certainly nowhere near London, which is probably a relief.'

'I wish she had come to us at Nettleford Park.

We would have certainly helped her.' Esther looked worried.

'She did not seek help from anyone. She tried to deal with it all by herself.' Phillip could hear the frustration in his voice as he told Esther this.

'Well, everyone has their own way of dealing with difficulties, I think, and Willa has never had anyone she could trust before at her side. Yet her strength is a great part of her attraction.'

Esther was right, Phillip thought. He'd loved her certainty and the way she strode through her life. She was neither a woman who dragged others down nor was she one who expected others to prop her up, which was part of the reason she had ended up in this mess.

Phillip wanted to wrap his hands around the throat of Mr Simon St Claire but the trouble was that he too seemed to have disappeared and was nowhere to be found. The miles to London town seemed longer than usual and he just wished they could get there so he could begin the process of clearing Willa's name. If his was to be muddied in the process, then so be it. He had had so much worse before.

He glanced at his brother and his wife, their hands clasped together on the seat between them, their coupledom so very easily seen. A true marriage was not defined by a ring or a piece of paper. It was in the intent of attachment and inseparability. It lived in friendship and devotion too and in the thousands of small hours that built all the memories of life.

Gretel and he had not enriched their time together with other places and people and adventures. They had not stood up for each other either when things got difficult. Silence had ruled their lives and disappointment had followed.

In the short time he had known Willa she had dragged him through Society and made him fight for his place in it, and she had been selfless enough to leave when she saw all the things he might miss out on should she stay.

He ground his teeth together and hated that he did not know where she had gone or if she was safe. Had the disappeared Simon St Claire gone after her to exact his own form of retribution?

Nothing made sense any more. Nothing felt certain.

'We will find her.'

His brother's words were quietly said and Phillip nodded as finally the lights of London town appeared in the distance.

Phillip could smell gardenias as he walked into his bedchamber, and on his nightstand two of Willa's hairpins sat in a small ceramic bowl. He had found those after she had left the last night they had slept together, and placed them there. As a keepsake and also as a tangible reminder that she had existed.

The warm woollen rug he had wrapped her in was folded now, stiffly, at the bottom of the bed, all the other remnants of their lovemaking tidied away. But he was glad of her scent, still lingering.

'Where are you, Willa? Are you safe?' He whispered this to himself but even the quiet words unsettled him. He then crossed to his writing desk on the far side of the room to extract two sheets of paper as well as his pen and ink.

He would begin with arranging a meeting of his own lawyers and then he would send a letter to the McAllistair sisters in Royal Tunbridge Wells asking if the old ladies had seen her. Their address would be easy to access from the new occupant of their London town house.

After that he would track down Simon St Claire using all the means he had at hand, and he knew that money loosened tongues as nothing else did.

'I'll find you, you bastard, and I will ruin you.'

He tucked a knife he had brought back from America into the top of his boot and hid it under the fold of his sock. He'd got rid of his gun after the debacle with his brother but today was the first time he wished it back. If St Claire had hurt Willa in any way physically he would kill him, he swore he would. Making a supreme effort, he swallowed down the anger that was building within him, took the pen up and began his first letter.

Chapter Thirteen

Willa sat on the seat before a mirror in a bedchamber of the small inn she had rented on the coast beside the English Channel.

She felt sick, that was the trouble, and shaky, and any smell of food in the morning made her want to throw up. She missed Phillip. She missed their night-times. She missed talking to him and laughing and being happy. She did not feel herself. She felt scared and brittle and uncertain, and there were dark rings under both her eyes.

She wondered if perhaps she was dying of an ailment that had suddenly crept up on her. She was crying a lot, which was also unusual, and any knock at the door made her freeze.

She had been in this inn in the little village of Winchelsea for almost a month now and in all that time she had barely moved from her room.

Mrs Withers, the housekeeper, had been nothing

but kind, providing her with her meals and making certain her room was cleaned and the bedsheets changed.

Willa had just felt exhausted and sick, her stomach churning and black spots appearing in her eyes if she tried to do too much. And so she had not. She had sat here looking out of the window at the river, the Brede, it was called, the last river flowing there after a storm centuries before that had washed all the others away.

The drowned old town was under the sea off the shale banks. Sometimes Willa saw the upward arms of old pieces of rock and stone if the tide was right. She liked looking for them, this history, because she felt a kindred spirit with the ruins drowning more and more, year on year.

Phillip.

She said the name less and less now to protect herself, though she dreamed of him every single night. Of them, together, making love in the moonlight.

Where would he be? Enjoying a life at Elmsworth, she hoped. Tending to his land. Or in London still, cursing her probably and hoping to never see her again after all her lies.

She could not help it. She had protected him and if that was all she could do for him she would be forever thankful. But her life had stopped and the money she had brought with her was running low. Soon she would have to decide what to do and where to go.

That thought brought on terror because she just could not decide, and the effort of leaving and moving on was too much to handle.

When the housekeeper came with a light lunch at noon, Willa thanked the woman as she smiled.

'You have been a wonderful help to me, Mrs Withers, and I hate to think what I might have done without you.'

Putting the plate of food on the small bedside table, Mrs Withers pulled a chair from the other side of the room and sat down. She had never done this before; usually she came in quickly and left just as quickly, a woman with all the chores of a busy inn sitting on her shoulders. So Willa was surprised by her tarrying.

'Might I talk with you for a moment, Mrs St Claire, woman to woman like? A moment just between ourselves?' She waited until Willa nodded before going on. 'Is your husband an abusive man? Is it him you are running from, my dear?'

'My husband died over two years ago, Mrs Withers. I am a widow.' This seemed to take the wind from the housekeeper's sails and she sat back, her teeth worrying her top lip in the motion of someone most nonplussed.

'Then perhaps a lover, my dear, for I think this sickness you have is almost certainly coming from the effects of early pregnancy.'

The world caved in around Willa and she could barely breathe, but Mrs Withers carried on. 'There is no shame in a love affair to my thinking, and any child is a gift, but your family might be worrying for you…'

'I have no family.'

A small smile creased the woman's lips. 'Well, maybe that's about to change, my dear, because you will have one in about seven months, I would say.'

'But I am barren. I have always known that I am.'

'Who told you that? A man, I would bet, and one that was probably infertile himself. It's how the world works. Men protect men and women protect women.'

Lionel and Lionel's doctor, a strict old man of strong beliefs. She remembered their telling her it was so in the dark sombreness of her husband's office and she had never questioned it. Barren Willa. Doomed to never carry a child. Infertile Willa. A burden on a husband who would want progeny. Sad Willa, stripped of any hope of a happier future.

Tears ran down her cheek in runnels and, using

the back of her hand, she wiped them away. Could it be true? Could such a marvellous thing be possible?

'There, there, dearie. It's not all that bad. You seem a learned woman who could no doubt find work to support yourself and the wee one. I could ask around the village if you like to see if there is an opening?'

Willa shook her head as she thanked the woman. 'Is there anything I need to be doing to make certain this baby stays safe?' Suddenly it was important that she know everything.

'Nothing. Rest, food and drink is the answer. The first three months are the worst and after that it all gets better and better. The last three months you will be tired but the middle ones are wonderful. Well, t'was so with my three, at least.'

At that Mrs Withers stood and placed the chair she'd sat on back in the spot she had moved it from.

'I ought to have said something to you before this, Mrs St Claire, but I did not quite know how to approach it and you never said anything at all of it.'

'I thought I was simply sick. I worried I might die.'

'Well, now you can relax a little and if there are things you need you just have to ask me.'

'Thank you.'

When she had left the room Willa stood and walked to the window, looking at her reflection in the glass. There was only a small face mirror here in this room and this was the best way she could see all of herself. Pulling her light cotton dress over her stomach, she fancied she saw a slight rounding, the shape of the tiny person who now lived inside of her.

Phillip's and her child. The child of Elmsworth that had never been expected. Panic settled next. What would happen when she birthed the baby? She was a woman with a difficult past and an uncertain future. If Phillip did not want her in his life after Simon St Claire's accusations became public, which she was sure that they would, might he try to take the baby? Should she even tell him of this pregnancy because with every fibre of her body she knew right then and there that she would never give the child up. Never.

Her hand rested on her stomach, different now to her from the way it had been even a quarter of an hour ago and her worries just fell away in the light of this amazing truth.

A mother. She would be a mother.

She remembered back to when she had told Phillip that she was barren after making love. He had been pleased with the news, wanting no complications and no extra worries. A simple, easy and sensual life, was what he had said, and they had laughed about it.

Now she felt so very different, and if he did not…?

She would have to tell him, she thought next, because it would be wrong not to, had to make him believe this child was not a trap but a choice. Her choice and if he made a different one then so be it.

Phillip. His smile. His silvered blue eyes. The delight they had shared together night after night. Every time she thought of him her heart broke just a little bit more.

'Please let it be all right. Please let things become better.' She whispered these words over and over again as she gazed out at the sea, rough from the wind and dark.

Chapter Fourteen

Six days later Phillip and Oliver finally found Simon St Claire. He was sitting at a table drinking with a small group of other men at the very back of the Red Hen Inn on the outskirts of Winchester.

Phillip ordered a drink and watched St Claire preen and pontificate, the words he spoke at such a volume they easily reached him here.

'Here's to the riches of the returned Belton Park, and may it long keep supplying me with money.'

A loud cheer went up all around him and Oliver swore roundly. 'He is too stupid to even recognise any danger.'

'This isn't the moment to take him.' Phillip's voice was firm. 'We will wait until he is properly drunk and away from the others.'

'Will he know us?' Oliver spoke softly.

'In these clothes? I doubt it.'

They had dressed for the part, in farmers' attire

they'd sourced from the tenants at Elmsworth, the hats on their heads largely obscuring their faces. They'd toned down their voices, too, in the way they had done as children, the rough brogue of Hampshire much more suitable in this setting.

Phillip had to admit that the disguise was a good one and it would take a keen eye and ear to determine their true identities. Hence they sat for an hour on their drinks and waited till a few of the others had made their way home and Simon St Claire excused himself to go outside.

Following him, they made their way over to the line of bushes which St Claire was relieving himself into.

'Mr Simon St Claire?'

The man turned and buttoned himself up.

'Who's wanting to know?'

In two seconds Phillip had crossed the space between them and dragged the man further into the bush, his arm firmly around the other's neck as he pulled him backwards, choking. Once out of earshot, he stopped and threw St Claire to the ground.

'Where is she? Where is Mrs Wilhelmina St Claire?'

The man grovelled and tried to stand but Phillip kicked him back down.

'Don't get up. Now, where is she?'

St Claire looked frightened, the cockerel inside diminished into a pale, uncertain man. 'I last saw Mrs St Claire in Royal Tunbridge Wells. She signed the documents for the rightful return of the Belton Park estate, but when I turned my back she ran away and I swear I never saw her again. I swear it on the name of my mother. Who are you?'

Phillip removed his hat.

'Elmsworth.'

Shock now showed in the other man's eyes.

'I never hurt her. I swear I didn't. I was playing a game, you see, so she would sign the document and I could leave.'

'Cease.' Phillip heard the words as if from a distance, the thrumming heat of anger burning into everything as he thought of how Wilhelmina must have felt at that moment. 'You are ruined, St Claire. Your accusations have all been debunked by those whom you threatened into helping you, so the only decent thing you can do now is to issue an apology and disappear from Society forever. Do you understand?'

The sound of voices became louder and the three men who had been sitting with St Claire in the tavern pushed through the undergrowth, their fists up.

Oliver hit the first one and downed him and Phillip took out the next man. The last two were harder, though Phillip managed to kick Simon St Claire in the face before he joined them in the fracas, and he lay unmoving on the ground.

Then Phillip crouched and went in low, the third man with the stick a heavier and more dangerous opponent. Still, he'd had these sort of fights in America and a lot of the memories surged back. He grabbed the weapon as it came down on the side of his chin and held his opponent on the ground.

Oliver had the fourth man on his knees, though there was a wicked bruising mark across his left eye where something had connected.

A moment later the local constabulary were there, called by those in the tavern, no doubt, and the questioning began. Within a few moments all of their assailants were hauled off. In relief Oliver and Phillip stood there looking at each other.

'A good afternoon's work, I'd say.' Oliver bent to retrieve his hat as he said this. 'Where the hell did you learn to fight like that, brother?'

'America. It was not an easy place to travel and I was still getting over Gretel's death.'

'We make a good team. You and I.'

Phillip began to laugh and something shifted inside him. Anger, hate, regrets and bitterness, he thought. They all seemed lessened somehow because he'd believed Simon St Claire when he'd told them he had not seen Wilhelmina after she had run from him.

Now all he had to do was to find out where the hell she had run to.

The cottage inhabited by the old McAllistair sisters in Royal Tunbridge Wells was set in a garden behind which stood a glade of trees, the birdsong loud as Phillip arrived the next evening.

The servant who answered the door took him through to a cosy parlour on one side of the hallway where the three McAllistair sisters were all arranged on their dainty chintz chairs, stiff drinks on the table before them.

'I am sorry to disturb you...' he began but was instantly interrupted by the shortest sister.

'Lord Elmsworth. Did you find her?' She was on her feet now, looking around behind him. 'Did you bring Willa back with you?'

The sister next to her was just as frantic when she saw he had not. 'She disappeared so suddenly and of course we have heard the very worrying rumours about her involvement in the death of her late husband, but they cannot possibly be true.'

'You are right and they are not. Mr Simon St Claire has rescinded every one of his accusations and apologised, and I have made sure that he will not trouble her again.'

'But where is she, then? Where has she gone to?' The third sister, with the glasses, finished her drink in one gulp after she had said this and frowned.

'That is why I am here. To ask you to tell me anything at all you remember Wilhelmina saying when you last saw her. Did she tell you of her direction? Did she have money on her? Did she need anything to take with her?'

The thinnest sister sat down and Phillip could tell she wanted to say something.

'I can help Wilhelmina and make sure that she is safe. I can find her.' He tempered his worry so that they might feel easier.

'Well, the day Willa came here she was in a state. Oh, she tried to hide it from us but we could tell she had been crying and all she had with her was her pelisse. No hat. No coat. Nothing. She said she had run from her rented house because a man had been there threatening her and she thought him dangerous. She said he imagined her to br a loose woman and had made the most unwanted advances.' Horror was reflected in opaque blue eyes.

'We gave her a coat and hat and a small suitcase with a few other things that we thought she might need. Jean tried to press some money into her hands but Wilhelmina said she had enough and would not require it. She sat with us for a few moments and had a drink and a sandwich and then she just got up and left.' A deeper frown marred her brow. 'We tried to rush after her but at our age any rushing is nigh on impossible and so we had to let her go.'

'And you have not heard from her since.'

The lady with the glasses shifted in her seat as she shook her head and looked nervous. 'I had a dream about her, my lord. I dreamt she was in a house in a block of other houses, a stone house by a river port. She was lying on the bed in her clothes in the middle of the day and the window was open. There were wooded hills behind.'

'Do you often have these sort of dreams?' Phillip was worried enough not to dismiss anything.

'She does, my lord.' The older sister spoke again. 'And they very often come true. Our mother was the same. We are used to it.'

'Did she say anything in your dream?' His words were quiet as he addressed the woman with the glasses.

'She said she needed help, my lord, because she is sick.'

A cold shiver went down Phillip's back and he stood up. 'Then I need to find her, ladies, and I will let you all know the minute that I do. Thank you. You have been most helpful.'

Once back on his horse he made for the tavern he had been staying in on the main street. He had seen a book of maps in the public room there and remarked upon the quality of the drawings in it, and the publican had said it was of the areas around Royal Tunbridge Wells down to the southern coast. Recalling his last conversation with Willa at his London town house, he wondered if she'd really meant it when she'd mentioned travelling to Europe? Praying she'd yet to secure any sort of passage to France, he tied his horse up outside the tavern.

The publican fetched the book of maps and sat down with him, listening as Phillip began to explain.

'I am trying to find a stone house on a river port which has hills of woodlands behind. It is somewhere near a village or a town and reachable by road from here.'

'Are you thinking of buying land around those parts, my lord?'

'No, I am trying to locate an old friend with whom I have lost touch. They wrote in a letter about the place but I cannot for the life of me remember the name.'

Phillip did not want to make this public. He wanted to make a quiet search without any news of it getting back to anyone. At first at least. If he could not find Wilhelmina by doing it this way, he would widen his parameters and get whoever he needed to be involved.

'You might try the outskirts of Hastings or even Winchelsea on Rye Bay. From memory there were houses there near the port with wooded hills behind. My father used to take us down there on his dray for a day or two before the hay making, you see, and a prettier place than that would be hard to find. Not too many people, mind, and not like them places near Brighton, full of the city folks at any time of the year.'

Which was why Wilhelmina would not have travelled west, he thought, and his eyes found Winchelsea settled on a large bay before a point.

Could this be at least a start? He looked further east and wondered if Willa had instead made for Folkestone or Dover. Perhaps she had intended to cross to Calais and escape entirely. If she had done that he would never find her, so he had to believe she was still in England.

But this was all conjecture. Closing the book, he thanked the publican and ordered a meal and a drink. He would get up early and begin his search, and he just had to pray that the dream the sister with the glasses had related to him was neither foolish nor fantasy.

* * *

Hastings was a busy town, a market stretching down the aptly named Market Street all along the road and selling every article of food, clothing, tools and home-ware possible.

After making his way to George Street Phillip paid for a room in the Royal Albion public house and left his baggage there. He would have a quick look around before he left for Winchelsea, for, with no true river port here in Hastings, he was eager to move along. The McAllistair sister had stated it was a river port she had seen in her dream, with wooded hills behind, and that did not fit the description of this place at all.

For a second he frowned because he could never have imagined himself chasing down dream houses with such a sincerity and putting so much hope on a fantasy.

'Please let me find her,' he said to himself over and over again. 'Please let her come safely home.'

It was all he could think of, Willa's fear, and her crazy notion that she might protect him by fleeing.

With Simon St Claire being dealt with by the constabulary up in Hampshire he at least had that worry off his mind. The man would never come near Wilhelmina again, Phillip swore on that soundly.

Two and a half hours later he rode into the port

village of Winchelsea, past an ancient gate that stood across the road, its adjoining walls long gone. The town itself was on a hill, with salt marshes before it. There was a large church in the middle of a gridded pattern of streets and Phillip turned towards the outer edge of the place to where it overlooked the river.

There was a number of small stone houses on this point and an inn that had rooms for rent. If anyone were to venture to Winchelsea to find a room this would be a good spot to start.

Knocking on the door of the inn, he waited. A stout older woman opened the portal and looked at him closely. She was wearing a clean white apron with a cloth hat of sorts tied around her head, and she looked at him warily.

'Can I help you, sir?'

'I am looking for a friend, Mrs Wilhelmina St Claire. Would she by chance be residing here?'

The woman said neither yes nor no but stood back and asked another question.

'And what name would I give her if she were here?'

'Mr Phillip Moreland.'

Could it be this easy? Had he chanced on the right place so quickly? He looked around, the river snaking behind, and a group of trees nearby. The hills at the back of the town were wooded.

'I will go and ask if she is a guest here.'

Turning, she shut the door behind her, leaving him standing there waiting.

A knock at the door had Willa tensing and when it opened Mrs Withers' head appeared.

'I am sorry to bother you, my dear, but there is a gentleman downstairs asking for you.'

The blood drained from Willa's face. Simon St Claire had found her. He was here in Winchelsea to take her back to the courts in London and he would surely rape her on the way. With a small breath of utter fright, she fell back onto the soft mattress of the bed behind her and fainted.

The hope that had risen in Phillip was dashed as the woman returned quickly and shook her head.

'I am sorry, sir, there is no one of that name residing here. Perhaps you might try the inn opposite the big church in the middle of the village. They cater for many guests and your friend may indeed be there.'

'Thank you. I will be at the Royal Albion in Hastings until the morning if you do hear Mrs St Claire has been in Winchelsea, and I will pay you well for any information.'

He slipped her a gold coin to sweeten the possibility of something coming from this contact but she only smiled and nodded, watching as he mounted his horse and rode away.

That evening, back in Hastings, Phillip knew he had come to a dead end. He would leave tomorrow to make for Folkestone and hope there would be some luck, and then he would go further east to Dover. There were so many places that Willa could be, so many bays and towns and villages in this part of England. So many farms, too. He poured himself another brandy because frustration had engulfed him and because he had left this morning with so much hope it felt deflating to be back here right where he had begun.

But he had felt close to Willa in Winchelsea. He had imagined her there in the inn by the river, watching, waiting and hoping. When he passed by tomorrow he would call in again, just to ask if perhaps the older woman had remembered anything because there had been some quick expression on her face that he was unsure about.

The brandy settled him and the food the publican had brought up was welcomed because he was tired from all his hours of riding.

Tomorrow would be easier, though, for he knew the way. Outside, the moon was bright and almost full. Phillip wondered if Willa was watching the sky, too, from her room over the river. The dream was beginning to feel like a truth to him, a way to find her, and he was glad of it.

It was dark and Willa could not settle.

The moon was nearly full tonight, a bright, wide orb in the sky. She had slept most of the day, a nightmare-filled slumber where Simon St Claire had her in his grasp and she could not get away.

When she had woken from her faint she had felt even worse than usual. The housekeeper had arrived back after a few moments with extra pillows for beneath her legs and with a tall glass of something that had made her sleep all day long until now.

'He is gone, my dear; he will not trouble you again. He has left for Hastings.'

Willa had not wished to ask anything at all about him this morning but tonight she felt braver.

'Did the stranger give you his name, Mrs Withers?'

'Mr Phillip Moreland.'

Wilhelmina's mouth fell open and she sat up, her legs dangling over the bed.

'I have to let him know that I am here.' She burst into tears as she said this, desperation building and hope too.

He had found her. He had come after her. She was certain Lionel's cousin must have spread his rumours about her by now, but even if Phillip had heard about all her past problems and all her questionable decisions he had still tried to find her.

'Mr Moreland gave me a gold coin for my trouble and asked me to get in contact with him if I remembered anything else. He said he would be at the Royal Albion there. He also said he would come by again tomorrow just in case I had more news. Is he your lover, dearie? Is he the father of your child?'

'He is.' Wilhelmina found a handkerchief and wiped her eyes and blew her nose. Worry set in across the face of the other woman.

'I thought he was the man you were scared of, the one you told me of when you first came here, but we can fix things up. I will have one of the boys go very early in the morning to Hastings with a note to ask Mr Moreland to call in here.'

'Thank you.'

'But for now you must eat something wholesome, so I have brought you a hot meal.'

Chapter Fifteen

Phillip knocked again at the door of the small Inn in Winchelsea. A note had been delivered early this morning asking him to return to the inn as soon as he was able to and he had saddled his horse immediately and left.

When the same woman he'd seen yesterday appeared, he smiled at her. 'I was pleased to get your note. Where is Mrs St Claire?'

'She is upstairs, sir, but she has been very ill.'

'What is wrong with her? Has a doctor seen her?' Panic filled Phillip. What could be wrong with Willa?

'She did not wish for one to be called at all, but if you follow me I will take you to her.'

The stairs were steep and narrow and the way was dark. When they reached the top the woman, Mrs Withers knocked on the door and then opened it.

'I shall leave you with Mrs St Claire, sir. She has requested for privacy.'

Phillip took three steps and saw Willa sitting on the bed, so much thinner than she had been when he'd last seen her in London and so very pale. She looked broken and beaten and crushed.

'What happened to your face?' Her first words startled him.

'I was in a fight with Simon St Claire.'

A slight smile crossed her face. 'But you dealt with him.'

'I did. He has taken back all his accusations against you and apologised. He has returned to his home in the north and I have warned him that I never want to see him again. I think he understood the true extent of my feelings and will venture nowhere near London or Hampshire again.'

She nodded and looked away and Phillip did not quite know what to say next. Wilhelmina looked so ill and brittle and so very small.

'I have been sick.' Her words were soft.

'I can see.'

She nodded again. There was a window beside her bed looking over the river. This reunion was nothing like the one he had imagined.

'How did you find me?'

'I went to visit the McAllistair sisters and the sister with the glasses told me she had had a dream that you were in a house overlooking a river port with wooded hills behind it. She was very convincing.'

His glance went to the view and he saw exactly what the old lady had imagined in her dream.

'That is Mildred.'

'Why did you did not wish to see me yesterday, or did you not receive the message?' He said this quietly in an attempt to understand her reasoning.

'I thought it was Simon St Claire who had come to call.'

Phillip crossed the room to be nearer to her but still he could not touch her. 'I gave my name.'

'The woman you spoke to, Mrs Withers, gave me a sleeping draught after I fainted and so I only learnt of your visit much later when I woke. A boy was dispatched to Hastings this morning with a note.'

She spoke slowly, none of her usual spark on display.

'Why did you run, Willa? Why did you tell me that our relationship had to end? Why did you not trust me enough to protect you?'

Her hand came up to her mouth and she bit at a nail. 'Because no one before you ever has, and I did not wish to ruin your life.'

'Will you come home to Elmsworth Manor with me? It will be safe there.'

'Yes.'

He could see that she was exhausted, the dark rings under her eyes a further worry. He would not hurry her and burden her with all the arrangements he was mulling over in his head to get her back to Hampshire. Instead he only said a little of it.

'I will leave you now to find us a way to get home. I will return around the lunch hour.'

'You promise you will come back?'

'I do.'

At this she lay down and closed her eyes, and within a moment she was sleeping.

When Willa woke again she thought seeing him an hour ago might have been a dream. Phillip had been here, she told herself, but, seeing the expression on his face, she knew what he was thinking. He was thinking that she looked awful and was trying his very best to hide his shock. He was thinking that she was only a shadow of the sensual woman he had known not too many weeks ago and he did not quite know what to say. He was unsure of her and tentative. He had not come close at all.

And now he was gone again to find transport to take them both back to Elmsworth Manor.

She had fallen asleep in front of him, their conversation only half finished and the gap between them wide with uncertainty. He had not touched her but had stood a good few feet away from the bed. Willa thought of Gretel and her sickness and knew that she had reminded him of that time, when everything was hopeless and his world had changed.

She tried to keep her breathing calm but the big gulps of air she was taking were anything but that. Tears ran down her cheeks, falling on the sheets and darkening the spots where they fell on the cotton.

She could not make herself feel anything except for sadness. The sensual days and nights in London felt like a dream, as if they had happened to someone else, not to her. She felt no wish at all to talk about their baby, safe inside her and hidden, the only part of her that she was certain of.

Perhaps Phillip would not come back. Perhaps he had mounted his horse and left for good, with his bruised face and knuckles. She was too much of a bother, too much hard work, and it was better to sever all ties and return to a life that was easier.

She shook her head and blew her nose.

No, he was too honourable to do that, and therein was the crux of the sadness of it all.

Two days later they were at Elmsworth Manor. The journey home to Hampshire had been a difficult and arduous one but now Willa was finally tucked up in a bedroom just down the hall from Phillip's.

He had told her that they'd always called it the Rose Room, both for the rose that climbed up the front facade and because during a summer sunset the whole room glowed pink.

When she woke again Phillip was sitting on a chair next to her bed, his long legs stretched out before him.

'Thank you for bringing me here.' Her voice was weak.

His head turned and he met her eyes. 'How do you feel? It was a long journey.'

She smiled at him, seeing his worry. 'I am tired after the travel but…better, I think. For the first time in ages I feel hungry, which must be a good sign.'

With a fresh nightgown on and her hair brushed Phillip thought that she did indeed look better. She was still far too thin, and the dark circles under her eyes were as easy to see, but her smile looked happier.

'I will ask the housekeeper to bring you up a meal and tomorrow I shall send for the Elmsworth physician. There may be medicines he could supply that we do not have here.'

She shook her head. 'No, I don't want him to examine me. I just want to rest.'

'Very well.' He went to stand but she stopped him with a gesture.

'Could you just stay until I am asleep, for I have nightmares sometimes…?'

He sat back again. 'You are completely safe here, Wilhelmina. Simon St Claire will never come back, I swear it.'

'It's not that…' she began.

'Then what is it?'

Tears rolled down her cheeks as she looked at him. 'I dream I have lost you. I dream you are somewhere…gone.'

His breath caught. 'I am here and I shall be here until you ask me to go.'

'I won't.'

But she was asleep already, in that strange way that she managed now. One moment wide awake and the next in full slumber.

'You did before,' he whispered when he was certain she would not hear.

He sat there until the moon was high and the sounds outside were quieter. Then he walked to the window and looked out.

'Thank you for letting me bring her home.' Whether it was God he thanked or the land around him or the whisper of ancestors he could always feel at Elmsworth, he did not know.

But Wilhelmina was home with him and she was safe.

* * *

His housekeeper came down to see Phillip in his study the next morning just after nine.

'Could I have a word with you, my lord?'

'I hope there is not a problem.'

'None, I assure you. Mrs St Claire is a perfect patient but it is a warm, sunny morning and I was wondering if you might walk with her outside for a little while.'

'You think her up to such an exertion?'

'We have located a wheelchair in one of the attics and have had it brought down. I think the sun on Mrs St Claire's skin and a bit of fresh air will be good for her. She has eaten some breakfast and the maid watching over her said her sleep, although broken, was also deep. Mrs St Claire has asked if it is possible for you to push her, Lord Elmsworth.'

At the front porch Phillip found Wilhelmina waiting there in the sun, face turned up to the rays and in a pretty yellow gown.

'I understand you would like to go out in the sunshine on this warm summer morning.'

'I would.'

'Then you will have me as your companion and we will begin in the garden.'

It was so beautiful here, Willa thought. Elmsworth Manor in the sunshine had turned into a different building altogether than the one she had left from in the rain and wind after kissing Phillip Moreland in his kitchen. Today the pale stone glowed in the light and the circular driveway was not full of puddles.

The gardens, too, were so much closer to the main body of the house than she had realised, for they surrounded the stone in a wild array of colour: the blue of cornflowers, the yellow of daisies and the white of a rose that scrambled over the portico, the same shade as the one outside her bedroom window.

It was joyous and uplifting and it was also fragrant. Willa breathed in and the perfumes engulfed her, warmed and potent in the morning sun. For the first time in weeks she felt…alive again.

He slowed down and turned the chair into an arbour of purple, the long blooms hanging down towards the soft green of the manicured lawn below.

A seat was placed beside it in the shade of small topiary bay trees and it was this he pushed her over to, positioning her chair at one end of the bench before sitting down next to her.

'This is the most beautiful garden I have ever seen.'

'My mother planted it and tended it. It was her masterpiece and so the gardener here has kept it up just as it was once years ago.'

'When she died?'

Leaning forward, he plucked a small blue cornflower from its stalk and handed it to her.

'Everyone has good times and bad times. Everyone makes mistakes. The thing is, my mother never learned from hers and so she made them over and over again. Not so much with plants but with people.'

'Were you one of those people?'

'Yes.' She saw the shock in his eyes and also the sorrow.

'Could I hold your hand?'

He did as she asked and she cradled it in her lap, her fingers tightly wound around his as if she might keep him from all his hurt.

Their first real touch since…

Pushing that thought away, she felt the sun and his warmth and the history of Elmsworth all around her. The world kept turning despite all that had happened and it was comforting that it did. She hadn't trusted him enough to help her but perhaps this small truce marked a beginning here in the garden of his mother.

Closing her eyes then, she slept.

Phillip did not move. He didn't pull his hand away either because in all the hours of searching for her he had not thought this sort of closeness would ever be his again.

He simply watched her. He watched the way the

small curls at her hairline blew in the wind and the peaceful expression on her face. He saw how the black circles under her eyes were actually a dark blue, like bruises from sickness, and that her nails, usually so short, had grown.

These weeks apart had changed them both and they were tiptoeing around one another trying to regain what they had lost. He could feel her reticence and he knew his wariness. Their balance was gone and in its place sat a carefulness that allowed nothing meaningful.

Rock the boat and you might lose everything. Yet they were losing it anyway in their refusal to discuss what had happened.

But she was sick and he was angry. For now, this was all it could be. The pounding, chaotic ecstasy was gone and in its place was uncertainty.

He tightened his grip just a little on her hand, careful not to wake her.

Oliver and Esther arrived just after five o'clock that evening and they were eager to find out just how Wilhelmina was.

'She has been ill and she goes in and out of slumber all day and night. She has nightmares and the maid says she cries a lot.'

'She has had a huge fright, Phillip. When I was

pilloried by all of Society after the truth about my mother came out at a public ball I was just the same. I was simply too scared to do anything at all, so I cried and I slept.'

'Did Simon St Claire hurt her?' Oliver asked this.

'It seems he tried to but she escaped and somehow got herself alone down to the south coast.'

'Has she told you about her journey?'

'She's struggling to speak much at all and I don't want to upset her by asking. She can barely cope with niceties.'

'Then she needs time,' Esther said this with certainty, 'and she does not need to be pushed. She needs patience to learn to trust again.'

'She's lost a lot of weight but I think she is eating more every day.'

'Aunt Julia sent a letter to Nettleford Park yesterday and she said that London Society was agog with the scandal of the St Claires and that many voices were not kind. I am not sure if she can ever go back to her old life, Phillip.'

'I am not, either, but right now she just needs to get better.'

'Has our physician been called?' This was from Oliver.

'Willa does not want him here. She is more than happy with how things are.'

'I can be a chaperone if it would help silence some of the detractors, Phillip.' Esther looked worried.

'No. It stays as it is.'

He saw his brother and sister-in-law glance at each other.

'There may be consequences from such an action.'

'I will deal with those if and when they come.'

'Then good luck to you, brother, though I doubt if you will need it. You seem to have come through a baptism of fire quite whole apart from the bruise on your chin. It suits you, such a mark. It makes you look as dangerous as I am finding out you are. America for all its faults and sadness has tempered you in steel and brought back a different man than the one who left the shores of England.'

'I do not think it was America, Oliver.' Phillip's words were quiet.

'It is Wilhelmina?' Esther looked delighted as she clapped her hands.

But he did not answer, turning to the cabinet in the corner and pouring them all a brandy. He needed the strength of it to get through this. But most of all he needed Willa well again.

Phillip walked with Willa slowly to his stables the next day and from the moment of being in the company of his horses she looked better.

'I think animals know when someone loves them,' he said quietly as her hands wandered over the nose of the next horse she was entranced by, her whole body alive.

Today she did not look sleepy at all, a new energy engulfing her every movement as she asked the horses' names and ages and background.

'How many do you keep here at Elmsworth?'

'Only around ten or so but I will build up that number now that I am home. My father stabled twenty or more and he won a few cups at the local competitions.'

'How wonderful.' She laughed and such unexpected joy had him staring at her.

'You are sounding so much happier.'

'That is because I am.'

'Oliver and Esther were here at Elmsworth last evening but they did not wish to disturb you.'

'Oh, I would like to see them next time they come.'

'I imagine it will be soon. Esther was full of questions though, so be prepared for that.'

'And you are not?' Her smile was kind.

'I was waiting until you were stronger, but I would like to know how you got down to Hastings undetected.'

'I went south because I thought Simon St Claire would probably go north. I hitched a ride with a family who were returning to Hastings. They dropped me off in the middle of the market town, where I purchased some basic clothing and Mrs Withers was there at the same stall and approached me to ask if I needed a place to stay. When I said I did she took me on the dray from the inn with all the week's produce and so I gained a room at Winchelsea.'

'I had imagined so much worse when you couldn't be found. I thought Simon St Claire might have kidnapped you.'

'I think he would have if I hadn't run.'

It was the first time they had had an honest conversation since he had found her again, Phillip thought. It was the first time they had looked each other fully in the eye, too.

'I know that I cannot return again to Society in London, so I was thinking when I feel better that I should like to rent a small house by the sea with a garden.'

He nodded and felt disappointment rise because every word precluded a future between them.

But she kept going, as he did not speak. 'I am an outcast now and I have no fight left in me to be otherwise.'

'There are options…' She didn't let him go on.

'All of which will keep me at the will or grace of others, don't you see? Simon St Claire has the house and land at Belton Park and there is very little left. I now want to make my life away from rumour and censure in a smaller and quieter way.'

She looked tired and much less robust than she had a few moments ago. Her hands twisted the material of her skirt this way and that. Phillip wished he could have stepped forward and laid his own over them, but her words sounded final. Once not so long ago he would have brought her up into his arms and whispered things to make it all better, but now…

Now they were two people whose path had forked and who had not pledged enough to each other before all of this had happened.

If he could go back and start again, what could he have promised? What would she have accepted? He watched her now leaning against the wall.

She had fought for him at the Kellands' ball when the Society gossip had pointed their arrows at him. But this was another matter entirely. Here they were both vigilant and wary.

Willa had tried so hard to stay awake after the visit to the stables but she had not managed it and the second she had lain down on her bed in her room she had been asleep. Glancing at the clock in the corner, she saw it was now late afternoon, the shadows from the day sloping onto her sheets.

She had to let Phillip go and her words in the stables had allowed him an escape. He had taken it. He did not need to feel responsible for her or obliged to offer help and she hated both her weakness and her sadness.

Her hands came across her stomach and she breathed in Elmsworth. This is your heritage, little one, she thought, your family that has inhabited this land for centuries. Your father is the eighth Earl of Elmsworth and if you are a boy you will be the ninth. Tears came to her eyes because a place in the world was important for everyone and as a child growing up she had seldom felt any sort of belonging.

Here the future stretched ahead and the past bolstered it up with all the portraits that marched down the main corridors. Every pale crenulated stone that made up the manor echoed of belonging as did the majestic oaks dotting the land around Elmsworth like sentinels.

This baby would be born into the lineage of men and women who had lived through the centuries as Morelands and as guardians of the earldom.

Yet she and Phillip were distant, both stung by the words she had delivered to him under the name of protection. Only an interlude. Just a dalliance. Leaving her no idea as to how she could break through the lies with truth.

She loved him.

She had always loved him.

Tears trickled down the side of her face and the sunset turned the room to the palest shade of rose.

She was surprised when a few moments later Phillip walked through the door of her bedroom and asked if he could have a few private words with her.

Without a second of hesitation she nodded.

'I hope you were able to sleep.'

'I was, thank you. Is everything all right?'

She sat up as he strode up and down before the window, not speaking until it seemed he had gathered his thoughts. But he did not look pleased at all.

'I have had time to think about your words today, the ones where you said you would not be a burden on anyone and about forging your own pathway.'

She stayed quiet.

'You see, the thing is, Wilhelmina, you have left me no room to state my case as to how I feel about this and I have been hesitant to do so because of your ill-health.'

'I don't expect pity.'

'You have told me that.'

'Or charity.'

'That too.'

'But I think we came into our relationship from

the wrong angle. We wanted delight and we got it, but we also created a distance that left nothing else available.'

'I don't understand.'

'I want to court you properly. I want us to get to know each other in ways different than we have. I want to find out if our compatibility is as good out of bed as it is in it.'

She bit her lip and looked at him. 'I am a poor choice for anything permanent. I have no dowry, no lineage and a ruined reputation which can only harm yours.'

'And I have told you that I need neither money, lineage, reputation nor protection.'

'What is it you do need, then?'

'I need a chance.' This time she smiled. 'I will take you out on day trips. I could make arrangements for a meal or a visit to friends. I would kiss your hand at the end of the day and say goodnight. I would not tumble you into my bed and promise nothing save sex as I did before.'

'That is a large honesty.'

'I think that we need it.'

'I do, too.'

A great bunch of summer flowers was brought to her room the next morning and the card attached had Phillip's name on it. When Willa was bathed and dressed he came to her door and asked if she would like to see the ballroom at Elmsworth.

'You have one here?'

'My great-grandfather had it added towards the back of the house because his wife loved to dance.'

'A thoughtful husband, then.'

Without hesitating further they began down the stairs. Surprisingly it was easy and it was not long until they walked through double doors into a huge room with polished wooden floorboards and high ceilings. Light streamed in through windows down one entire and long side.

'Did you have balls here when you were young?'

'No. I never remember it being used even once, but then, my mother was not a woman who enjoyed frivolity or crowds.'

'And Gretel…did she not wish to make Elmsworth come alive with the joy of it all?'

'She didn't. This is the first time I have been inside here for at least a decade.'

'It's so beautiful. I can imagine an orchestra over there and people dancing with great bunches of flowers from the Elmsworth gardens in vases around the room. If it was summer all the windows could be open and people could spill out into the gardens through those doors. I would have loved to see that.'

'You still could.'

'I am an outcast, remember. No one would come.'

'Dance with me, then. Just us.'

He offered her his hand and when she took it he began to count. On three he guided her across the floor towards the windows and then stopped.

She was glad that he did because even such a small movement had left her breathless, but she had managed it and just that thought gave her hope.

'This room makes you a better dancer, my lord.'

He laughed at that. 'We should practise more, then, but not today. Today there is tea and cake on the small porch off the library waiting to be eaten.'

'You have thought of everything.'

'I am trying, Wilhelmina.'

The blood came to her face because in truth the delight they had shared was still within her and close.

'Thank you for showing me this. I will never forget it.'

'Good.'

He tucked her hand into the crook of his arm and led her out into the sunshine.

She dreamt of him that night, of them in bed, without clothes and with hours before them. It was the first time in weeks that she had felt true interest in anything sensual.

Tomorrow he had promised her a trip in the carriage to see a local waterfall. Closing her eyes, she made herself stay very still and then she slept.

Chapter Sixteen

They sat on small folding stools Phillip had set up on flat ground opposite the waterfall. Water cascaded down stepped brown rocks to a river at the bottom. Green branches from trees marched up the hillock, mist from the water dampening their leaves.

Willa felt the mist on her face when the breeze came their way; a refreshing wetness that took away fatigue.

'It is very beautiful. Do you come here often?'

'I did when I was younger. It was a retreat.'

'From home?'

'From life, I think. From decisions and anxiety.' He hesitated before adding, 'From my mother. She was a difficult woman. A woman who had long periods of anger and melancholy.'

She saw him take in a breath and hold it, as if to calm himself before he went on.

'She tried to kill me and Oliver twice. The second

time was on the lake one late afternoon when she deliberately tipped us out of the boat in the deepest part. She had a knife and she used it when we tried to get back on the upturned hull.'

'The scars on your arm and back?'

He nodded. 'At other times she could be kind and almost gentle, though when she did hug us it always hurt, because she squeezed too hard.'

'Perhaps she was trying, through her sickness, to show you she cared. I read a book once about a man who said his illness was like a fog with only small glimpses of reality showing through. I imagine in those times your mother would have been desperate to make her love known to you, like a balancing act that she could never win, because she was a prisoner in her mind and with no way out.'

His smile was beautiful as he looked at her. 'And a sickness is not a choice?' There was a sort of relief in his words.

'It isn't, and we have to be grateful that we don't have such an affliction.'

'I used to think that I might be just like her because I was often sad.'

'I have yet to meet a person who wasn't sad sometimes, Phillip. It's simply part of life. I spent years at Belton Park trying my hardest to smile just so that I remembered the feeling, but places form you, don't they, and in ways that you never realise until you are gone from them? Belton Park made me more melancholy than I wanted to be and much more guarded. When I came to London I was lonely until I met you.'

His glance came up at the words and for a second she felt dizzy. He was there as he had been before, a burning awareness that was enthralling, a new beginning as the disconnection between them loosened.

He had promised her courtship and he was trying to deliver it. The distance between them was getting smaller and every truth they gave to each other held the power to heal. She listened as he kept talking.

'I learned the art of being reserved from Gretel and it was a mistake we both regretted in the end. The Perfect Match. The Union of the Season. Two people who were only meant for each other. That's what people said all the time and we tried to believe it ourselves until…all that was left were regrets. Hers and mine. She was beautiful but she was also difficult, and when she died I felt guilty about not being able to make her different and about not loving her enough. She said that in the end we didn't love each other enough.'

'Only those in a marriage know what happens there. It's what put me off the possibility of there ever being another one, though I doubt Lionel and I gave the impression of a perfect match. I sometimes wish I could do it all over again and get it right.'

'With Lionel?'

'No, certainly not.' Her laughter filled the small glade, tinkling like the water, the sound like music to his ears. Every day she was recovering a little more. He could see it in the tone of her skin and in the humour in her eyes. She was sleeping less lately, too, and conversations such as these took him back to the time before.

They had always been able to talk well together and laugh.

'In the winter this waterfall is much louder and the river spills over its banks onto the farmland below, forming a marsh that is filled with insect life.'

'I would like to see that.'

It was the first time she had allowed the hint of a future between them.

'I hope that you will. But now I think we should eat, for I have lunch in this basket.'

'You have been more than kind to me, Phillip.'

'And why should I not be, Willa?'

'Because I did not trust you enough to help me and I should have.'

'It was not all your fault. I had my part in it, too.'

The corners of her lips turned up.

* * *

That evening he came and sat with her by her bed. She had slept for an hour or so on their return from the waterfall but now that she was awake she looked excited about something.

'I feel so much better than I did, which is a huge relief.'

'I'm glad.'

She put out her hand to him and he placed his on top.

'Could you stay with me in bed tonight for a while? Not to…' She hesitated and did not finish. 'Just to sleep?'

'I'd like that.' He leant down to undo his shoes and took off his socks and jacket. Then he slipped across to lie on top of the coverlet, putting his arm out so that she snuggled up beside him, her head pressed in.

'You smell different. There are no gardenias.'

'I left my perfume in London and I miss it.'

'You smell…clean.'

She giggled. 'It's the soap that your housekeeper plies me with.'

Her breath was warm against his neck as she spoke.

'It feels safe here at Elmsworth. I can see why you like the manor because it is strong and beautiful and constant. I have never lived in a place that has felt this way before.'

'Steeped in history,' he returned. 'Oliver and Esther sent word today that they would like to come and visit the day after tomorrow. Would you feel up to that?'

'Yes, I would like to see them, but I wonder how they feel about me after what has happened?'

'Oh, I wouldn't worry. They have had their own battles with Society and survived. Perhaps it would be good for you to hear how they did it and then we could do the same.'

'We?'

'I'm here with you, Willa. I'm not going anywhere. I promise.'

'Thank you.'

He leant down and kissed the top of her head gently. Outside the stars were bright in an inky sky.

'You must show me which is your star one day.'

'In truth I can't remember where it is. Lionel's gesture was always only an empty one after all and I did not set much store by it.'

'Then let's choose another star and name it as our own.'

Her nod heartened him. 'We could do that and wish on it for good fortune. Do you know, without you I think I might have given up on life altogether?'

He shook his head. 'Given up? You? My brave warrior woman who can handle any situation with aplomb? I doubt it.'

She turned and kissed him then, on the lips with care and shyness, and his eyebrows rose.

'Would you like to have dinner with me tomorrow night, in the dining room?'

'A formal occasion? Just us?'

'I promised you a courtship, Wilhelmina. I will not rush you into anything else.'

Not even another kiss? she wanted to say, but she stayed silent. The joy at feeling better was building inside her and for the first time in weeks and weeks she wasn't bilious. Even the tiredness was diminishing and in its place came hope and excitement.

Phillip's warmth beside her was welcomed and the way he ran his fingers over her bare arm in a caress was wonderful.

Together. Here at Elmsworth Manor. She never wanted to leave. She wanted to stay here forever with him, away from others, away from censure.

Yet to live well they would have to take risks and confront those who were critical of them. But not right now, she thought next as she snuggled into him. Now they would lie here in the quiet darkness and simply be. She liked the way he had said he was not going anywhere, the protection of his family home and land all around them, and their little one growing inside her each day.

Willa dressed with care for dinner the next evening, in a simple gown that she had found in the Hastings marketplace before she had gone to Winchelsea.

She styled her hair herself, rolling it softly into a loose bun and securing it with very few pins.

When the clock in the corner beat out the time of half-past seven she took the flowered cotton frock from its hanger and pulled it over her head, securing the many small buttons and straightening the neckline.

Stretching the fabric of the skirt back against her stomach, she enjoyed the slight roundness before she let the fabric go.

Her cheeks were flushed and her eyes looked bright, the sick, wan woman gone and replaced by one who was blooming and radiant and happy.

She would tell Phillip about the baby this very evening but she would do it properly. She would tell him that she loved him first and had done so since the first moment of meeting him. She would hide nothing. He had always stressed the importance of honesty and so she would give that to him.

A quarter of an hour later there was a knock on

the door, and when she opened it Phillip Moreland stood there.

He wore cream breeches and a burgundy jacket under which he had donned a white shirt and neck cloth. His hair was slightly wet, slicked back into its unusual length, unbound today and inclined to curl.

He was beautiful. And unfamiliar. A suitor whom she would never have expected to have, a man who was incomparable, the weight of Society and tradition gathered in his footsteps.

'You look impossibly like an earl of the realm, my lord.'

He laughed at that and took her hand. 'And you look breathtakingly enchanting.' He reached into one of his pockets and brought out a small decorated bottle.

'This is for you.'

'Perfume with gardenias.' She clapped her hands.

'I had one of my men ride across to Winchester today and source it for you because you said that you missed the fragrance.'

'It is a perfect gift,' she said as she unstoppered the bottle to dab the oil on her wrists and neck, holding out her arm for him to smell.

Then he shepherded her down the wide mahogany staircase into the dining room filled with candles and flowers.

'Oh, it all looks so well put together. Did you ask for it to be like this?'

'I did. Everyone helped to make it special for you. The gardener, the cook, the housekeeper and the younger kitchen maids. They all wanted to please you.'

'And they have. I always imagined sitting down at a table dressed like this.'

'Then allow me to see you to your seat.' Pulling back one of the carved wooden dining chairs, he waited until she was comfortable and then took the chair next to her at the head of the table.

There was a bottle of wine standing before them and he poured two glasses, raising his own against hers.

'To health, then,' he said, 'and to happiness. You are looking stronger each day.'

'I am and it feels good to be sitting down here to eat a meal again and to be out of the sickroom. Are Oliver and Esther here at Elmsworth in the morning?'

'They are.'

'Will they stay the night?'

'Probably not. I don't think they are bringing their children over until they know you are recovered, so it's most likely just them.'

'I am so glad that you have resolved things with Oliver.'

'I have you in part to thank for that, for you made me see the importance of family.'

Should I tell him my news now? she thought, but it seemed odd to stuff such a momentous truth in between the main course and the dessert and so she kept silent. She needed a moment between them that was…romantic to begin her confession, but so far their chat had been mostly of other people and different situations.

However, as they finished the last bite of a delicious lemon cake with clotted cream Phillip took her hand into his and the tone completely changed.

'Would you consider coming to my room tonight, Willa, and not just to sleep?'

'I would.'

His smile was dazzling as she laid a finger across his mouth. 'Could we go up now?'

Now, before she lost both her chance and her courage.

She held on to his hand tightly all the way up the stairs and when he shepherded her through to his bedchamber she continued to hold it even after he shut the door.

How did one begin? she then thought wildly, taking in a breath to calm herself, but he was talking now and they were words that were most unexpected.

'I do not want to lose you again, Wilhelmina. I always thought it was a physical relationship that I needed until I could not find you, and then I knew I wanted so much more. I know this will come as a shock, given your position on never wanting to be married, but I cannot imagine a life without you and in all honesty I am not sure I could survive such a thing.'

Tears filled her eyes.

'I am trying to say that I love you, Wilhelmina, I love you so much that I am scared every moment we are apart.'

She moved close to him and wrapped her arms around his body.

'I love you, too, Phillip. I knew I did when we slept together that last time but I was frightened to tell you, and in Winchelsea without you I wanted to die because my heart was broken.'

She led him over to the bed and asked him to sit down. Then she stood back and unbuttoned her gown, pulling it off over her head with her petticoat before taking his hand again and placing it on her stomach.

'I'll love you always but you need to know things

are different now. For us. I am three months pregnant and that is why I have been so sick.'

His mouth fell open, his other hand coming up to cradle her stomach, and she saw him swallow twice before tears formed in his eyes.

'How can this be true? I thought…'

'Neither of us is infertile, Phillip. It was all a lie told to us by others.'

He could barely find his voice, this moment so very unexpected, all the beliefs he'd always held about himself beginning to unravel. They would have a child, an heir for Elmsworth and maybe by God's grace other children as well. The lineage would continue, the house and its land would be safe. A future beckoned that he had never considered or thought possible before. A miracle.

'When…will it come?'

'I think it will be March. I think he or she must have been conceived that night after the Kelland ball.'

'Our first night of delight?'

She laughed and he did too, recovering from the shock now and full of excitement.

'You are the only person I have ever been truly honest with, Willa, and the only one I trust completely. For the first time I can see a future here for me, for us, at Elmsworth, making our life.'

He then knelt before her and his hand sought hers, his radiant wife in her underclothes and sheer gartered stockings, the smell of gardenias in a cloud all around her.

'Would you marry me, Wilhelmina St Claire? Would you do me the honour of being my wife?'

'Yes.'

And then they were in each other's arms in the bed, his mouth tipping down to hers as he kissed her, deeply, completely and honestly. He held nothing back and neither did she.

His manhood rose but he was not certain if this would be safe.

'I want you.' Willa solved the dilemma for him, opening her legs and inviting him in.

'It will not hurt the baby…?'

She kissed any more words away and then the old magic between them was back, the passion and the desperation. And finally, again, the delight.

Epilogue

25th December 1820, Elmsworth Manor.

It was Christmas Day and they had spent the last five weeks readying Elmsworth Manor for all the glory of the upcoming Season.

Wilhelmina had never celebrated Christmas before, certainly not at Belton Park and not even in London. It had always been a day that others loved and one that she dreaded, but this December she and Phillip had made their plans early and carefully.

They had watched the cook make her Christmas puddings on Stir-Up Sunday and had handed out gold coins on the 21st December to those who were down on their luck in the parish.

The house was bedecked inside with gold and silver paper twisted into long running bands. Interspersed with this were small branches of pungent pine, ivy, laurel, hawthorn and bay all tied with shiny red ribbons. On the mantels there were pine cones, apples, oranges and holly berries on display.

'It looks most festive,' Phillip said beside her as they stood receiving their many guests in the front salon. 'But I think you need to look up, my love.'

When she did he swooped down and kissed her thoroughly and with purpose, the mistletoe ball hung most strategically at the open door they were under.

Oliver whooped in delight as he came to stand beside them with Esther.

'Who would have ever thought that my brother would have a love nest of his own to live in before he had been back in England for even a year?'

'Men need them to be happy,' Esther broke in. 'All women know that, don't they, Willa? Without a home and hearth men are like young birds naked in the cold.'

Wilhelmina laughed, thinking back to the time when she had tutored Phillip on exactly that subject.

'I imagine Phillip and Oliver might have a few more resources at hand than that of a lost chicklet, Esther, but…' She let the sentiment slide as Phillip pulled her closer.

Inside her their first child grew and moved and her hand cradled her stomach as she smiled. Their love nest was filling up.

Julia joined them next, hand in hand with Juliette, Oliver and Esther's daughter, and behind them trailed William, his mouth full of sweets that he had been told not to touch until after dinner.

'I think your parents would finally be at peace if they could have only seen you now, Phillip. I know that I most surely am and it warms my heart as your aunt.'

To one side in a corner Arabella Montague sat with the Duggans, the vibrant, happy girl of six months ago now a quiet, sullen one with a large scar across the bottom of her cheek. She had not spoken of what had happened to her and her father in France to anyone yet but they were all doing their very best to bring some of the Christmas cheer her way.

Mary Duggan saw them looking across and raised her glass to them, in a quiet gesture of thanks.

Willa took Phillip's hand, the ring on her finger sparkling in the light. They had married two months ago at the end of autumn because they did not have time to wait for the spring and because Phillip was adamant that she would be his wife as soon as possible.

'I love you,' she whispered and liked the smile he gave her in return.

Soon they would repair to the table filled with Christmas fare and they would sit and talk of this year's happenings and of next year's hopes.

But before they did that Phillip took a spoon and tapped it against the crystal of his glass, capturing everyone's attention.

'Thank you for coming to Elmsworth to enjoy Christmas together with us. For me this year has been one of discovery and wonder, all of which I can directly attribute to my wife, Wilhelmina. She has allowed me to find peace at Elmsworth, and purpose, and the sort of love that I could never have imagined.

'But family and friends have played their part, too, welcoming us in, supporting us when things were difficult and making sure that we are not alone here.

'Merry Christmas, everyone.' He raised his glass to drink and the others did the same.

Outside it was snowing and the world was becoming white, but in here the Yule log burned and the chatter all around drowned out the sounds of a strengthening wind.

They were safe here and home and later tonight she and Phillip would lie in the comfort of their large feather bed upstairs and find the centre of each other. It was all Willa had ever dreamed of and she felt a peace and joy that she had never known before.

At thirty-one she was radiantly happy and the sapphire ring Phillip had placed on the third finger of her left hand sparkled against the flame of the fire. Her birthstone in her marriage ring.

Love was everywhere now and she turned to smile at her husband, liking the way the blue in his eyes silvered in want as if he too was thinking of later; thinking of delight.

* * * * *

If you enjoyed this story, why not check out Sophia James's other great reads?

Their Marriage of Inconvenience
The Spinster's Scandalous Affair
The Debutante's Secret

And be sure to read her Gentlemen of Honour miniseries:

A Night of Secret Surrender
A Proposition for the Comte
The Cinderella Countess

MILLS & BOON®

Coming next month

THE MAID'S MASQUERADE
Catherine Tinley

Book 1 in **The Heiress Switch** series

'Why will you never speak of your mother, or our betrothal?' he asked, and her heart was sore at the sincerity in his eyes. 'You must know I wish you to be my wife.'

Marguerite could not help it; she allowed her eyes to show the feelings she must never give voice to.

'Sophia!' he cried, moving to kiss her, but she recoiled, his use of Sophia's name feeling like a slap in the face to Marguerite. 'What is it?' He paused, ever the gentleman.

'No. I—I must not! I am so sorry for leading you to believe…for even suggesting that I might… I cannot!'

'But why?' He took her hands. 'Can you not be honest with me?'

She winced. Honesty was the one gift she was not free to give.

'I have come to know and admire you very well these past weeks,' she began carefully, weighing every word. 'But there are things…there are matters which I am not free to discuss, my lord.'

'You should call me Benedict,' he offered, confusion clear in his expression, but she shook her head.

'It would not be right,' she said firmly. A servant should never, ever make use of the intimate name of a peer of the realm.

'You are a puzzle, Miss Van Bergen!' He ran a hand through his hair. 'A puzzle, and a damn—a *dashed*—paradox, and I know not what to make of you!'

His anger was clear, and suddenly it occurred to her that his own recovery from her betrayal might be expedited if she gave him a disgust of her. So, hardening her tone and lifting her chin, she shrugged. 'It is very simple, my lord. I have done what I needed to do in the pursuit of my own interests.'

Continue reading

THE MAID'S MASQUERADE
Catherine Tinley

Available next month
millsandboon.co.uk

FOUR BRAND NEW BOOKS FROM
MILLS & BOON MODERN

Indulge in desire, drama, and breathtaking romance – where passion knows no bounds!

OUT NOW

Eight Modern stories published every month, find them all at:

millsandboon.co.uk